Twin headlights bore down on Cody...

He leaped forward, then dived between his vehicle and the next, his right elbow striking the pavement. Pain shot through his arm and side.

When he got back onto his feet, Erin stood facing the street, pistol drawn. The car squealed onto Pine Island Road, its rear end fishtailing. Taillights shrank and disappeared as it sped away.

Erin lowered the weapon and ran toward Cody, panic in every line of her face. "Are you all right?"

He flexed his arm. "I'm sure my elbow's bruised, but it's not broken. Did you see the car?" As quickly as it happened, he didn't expect a tag number, but a description might help.

"I think it might have been the bomber's Camry, but in the dark I can't say for sure."

"I'm sorry. You were right." Cody wasn't too proud to admit when he'd messed up. He hadn't just put himself in danger. He'd endangered the lives of both Erin and her dog...

Carol J. Post writes fun and fast-paced inspirational romantic suspense stories and lives in sunshiny central Florida. She sings and plays the piano for her church and also enjoys sailing, hiking and camping—almost anything outdoors. Her daughters and grandkids live too far away for her liking, so she now pours all that nurturing into taking care of two fat and sassy cats and one highly spoiled dachshund.

Books by Carol J. Post

Love Inspired Suspense

Midnight Shadows
Motive for Murder
Out for Justice
Shattered Haven
Hidden Identity
Mistletoe Justice
Buried Memories
Reunited by Danger
Fatal Recall
Lethal Legacy
Bodyguard for Christmas
Dangerous Relations
Trailing a Killer

Visit the Author Profile page at Harlequin.com for more titles.

TRAILING A KILLER

CAROL J. POST

LOVE INSPIRED SUSPENSE
INSPIRATIONAL ROMANCE

LOVE INSPIRED® SUSPENSE
INSPIRATIONAL ROMANCE

ISBN-13: 978-1-335-40500-5

Trailing a Killer

Copyright © 2021 by Carol J. Post

Recycling programs for this product may not exist in your area.

This edition published by arrangement with Harlequin Books S.A.

For questions and comments about the quality of this book, please contact us at CustomerService@Harlequin.com.

Love Inspired
22 Adelaide St. West, 40th Floor
Toronto, Ontario M5H 4E3, Canada
www.Harlequin.com

Printed in U.S.A.

My grace is sufficient for thee:
for my strength is made perfect in weakness.
—2 Corinthians 12:9

Acknowledgments

Thank you to my uncle Danny Post, who showed us
around Matlacha and Pine Island and gave us
the inside knowledge that only a "local" can have.

Thanks to my sister, Kimberly Wolff, who not only helped
me plot this book but also let me drag her around
South Florida for research. You're the best sis ever!

Thank you to my editor, Dina Davis, and my
critique partners, Karen Fleming and Sabrina Jarema,
for making my stories the best they can be.

And thank you to my husband, Chris, for
keeping romance in my life for the past forty years.

ONE

Erin Jeffries moved down the two-lane road that spanned the eighteen-mile length of Pine Island. Sheets of rain slapped across the windshield, the final fury of a storm that had pounded the area for most of the night.

Ahead of her, a metal post stood at the edge of the sidewalk, devoid of whatever sign it had held yesterday, and stubborn fronds clung to battered palm trees. A hodgepodge of limbs, metal, wood and plastic littered the roadside.

Florida had seen worse. This one was only a category three, but it still packed enough punch to be dangerous. If the report she'd gotten was accurate, someone was trapped in the rubble of a building that had collapsed. He would probably come out of the experience with a new respect for Mother Nature. If he came out of it at all.

At the northernmost tip of the island, Erin navigated a gentle left turn. Charlotte Harbor lay to the right, invisible behind the rivers that flowed down her windows. She glanced in her rearview mirror. The top of a crate peeked over the back seat of her RAV4. Her white German shepherd was inside.

"Almost there, Alcee."

Maybe the current band of rain would move past them by the time they had to exit the vehicle. If not, she and Alcee would still do what they needed to. Emergency personnel ventured out as soon as conditions were safe, not necessarily comfortable.

Erin lifted her foot from the accelerator. Capt'n Con's Fish House lay to the left, and the grassy area beyond offered boat trailer parking. Main Street continued farther, but public access ended there. A sheriff's vehicle sat off the roadway, ensuring no one ventured past the no-trespassing sign. Erin could get through with her badge identifying her as a detective with the Lee County Sheriff's Office. But today she was acting in a different capacity.

As she drew to a stop, the deputy exited the vehicle, head tilted downward beneath the hood of his rain slicker. Erin cracked her window enough for conversation. The deputy had just started to give her a curt nod when a smile spread across his face.

She and Joe had started with Lee County a year ago, both in patrol. Nine months later she'd made detective, at least in part due to the glowing recommendation the department in Sunnyvale, California, had given her. Though their paths didn't cross that often, they'd stayed on friendly terms, friendly enough for Joe to keep trying to match her up with his former neighbor.

Joe glanced at the dog in the back. "I take it you're not on duty."

"Not with Lee County. Alcee and I are volunteers with Peace River K-9 Search and Rescue. We're looking for hurricane victims." One, anyway. She'd gotten the call right after daybreak and had been ready to respond within ten minutes.

"Every mandatory evacuation, there are always people who think the *mandatory* part of that phrase doesn't apply to them." He shook his head and, after wishing her success, waved her through.

Erin raised the window and crept past him. Her destination was on the last small street branching off Main, a large older home that had been converted to apartments.

She made a left onto Boca Vista and drove past the first residence. When she stopped behind the sheriff's vehicle sitting in the next drive, she released a low whistle. The building in front of her seemed to have tipped forward, the two upper stories falling onto the first. Rafters, joists and studs jutted outward from the jumble like broken bones.

Her hope that the rain would slack off by the time she arrived hadn't materialized. She reached for the slicker in the seat beside her. Alcee's search-and-rescue vest wouldn't do anything to keep her dry, but at least the big, fat drops weren't cold. Florida rain in August was just wet.

Erin shrugged into her raincoat. As she stepped from her car, a deputy rounded the corner of the house and called a greeting. She'd met him when she started with the department, but hadn't seen him since. They worked different shifts in different parts of the county. She struggled to pull up a name. Hidden beneath the rain slicker, his nameplate was no help.

"Erin, right?"

"You have a good memory." She gave him a sheepish smile. "Better than mine."

"I had just one name to learn. You had a whole department." He extended a hand. "Alan Drummond."

She accepted the handshake. "So what do we have?"

"I've only been here about fifteen minutes. We got the call from one of the residents in town who didn't evacuate. He got out at the crack of dawn, during one of the lulls." Drummond nodded toward a white Dodge Ram sitting next to the cruiser. "With the truck parked here, he's afraid someone might have been inside when this came down."

"Have you heard or seen anything?"

"Not a thing. I've circled the building, calling out, but haven't gotten a response."

"If anyone's there, Alcee will find them." She opened the back door of her SUV and unfastened the latch on the crate. "Come."

Alcee jumped out, undeterred by the pouring rain. Beneath the vest, eagerness rippled through her sleek body as if she sensed the importance of what she was about to do. Erin bent to scratch her neck and cheeks. "You're a good girl."

As Erin moved toward the wreckage, Alcee pranced next to her. The dog would do her work off leash.

Deputy Drummond followed. "We've been in touch with the owner of the building and are working on contacting his tenants. I ran the tag on the Ram, and it came back registered to someone in Cape Coral. I don't know why it's parked here, unless he moved and didn't update his address."

Erin pointed at the pile of rubble. "Seek."

The dog didn't hesitate. As she gingerly made her way upward, boards shifted under her, but she maintained her footing.

Erin's heart pounded. *God, please help her.* Working around collapsed buildings was dangerous, and dogs had been hurt. But it was more than that. She really wanted Alcee to succeed. Whoever might be trapped in that building *needed* Alcee to succeed.

The two of them had finished their search-and-rescue training a year and a half earlier, and although they'd participated in several searches for lost children and elderly people with dementia, the missing person had always been found in one of the other teams' grids. This time she and Alcee were alone. But the dog was ready. She'd practiced this scenario dozens of times, with a trainer hiding in rubble. She'd passed every test and graduated from the program.

Except this wasn't a simulation. It was the real thing, with a real life at stake.

Drummond watched the dog for several minutes, then returned to his vehicle. Erin stayed rooted to the spot, pleas for help circling through her mind. Her primary prayer was that there weren't any victims. Her follow-up was that if there were, help would reach them in time.

As she waited, the rain abated, then stopped altogether. Steel-gray clouds blanketed the sky, a small patch of brightness barely visible at the eastern edge. She slipped out of her rain jacket and laid it over the hood of her vehicle to dry. Maybe that last band was the end of it.

A rumble broke the silence, the distant sound of helicopter rotors beating the air. The volume and pitch increased as it grew closer. It was likely one of the local news stations.

She joined Drummond at his vehicle. "Anything new?"

"So far all the tenants are accounted for except a single, older gentleman. The calls go straight to voice mail. The Ram belongs to his grandson."

Erin nodded. "Maybe the grandson came to pick him up and they left in the grandfather's vehicle."

She returned her attention to her dog. Alcee's movements had grown more animated. She was sniffing with new vigor, head down, nose tracing a jagged path. She'd locked on to a scent.

Erin's pulse picked up speed, and her heart beat in her throat. Alcee's first find. At least, her first find that involved a real injured person, not a trainer pretending to be trapped.

The dog pawed at a board, released three barks and sat. That was her indication—bark and sit.

Erin turned to Drummond, unable to keep the tremor from her voice. "Alcee's found a survivor. We need debris-removal people."

"Already done. A construction company's on the way with a crane."

As if in response, the deep roar of an engine drifted to them. A half minute later a truck turned the corner, a crane mounted in its bed. Turner-Peterson Contractors, according to the sign on the door. She met the driver at the road.

"Someone's trapped, right up there."

She pointed to Alcee sitting atop the debris like a furry sentinel. She'd stay until Erin released her.

A pickup truck bearing the same signage as the first arrived. It remained parked at the road while the other driver maneuvered the crane truck into position.

Erin retrieved a rope toy from her vehicle and held it up. "Alcee, come."

The dog made her way down as carefully as she'd ascended. Erin couldn't tone down her smile. Warmth swelled inside her—love for her dog and pride in what she'd accomplished.

Less than three years ago Alcee was training to be a companion dog for the blind but wasn't getting it. They'd tried training her for narcotics detection, and that hadn't gone much better. Fortunately, her trainers had recognized that, with her curiosity, endless energy and toy drive, she was better suited to a search-and-rescue career.

Erin dropped to her knees and wrapped her arms around the dog. "Good girl." She held out the twisted rope with the ball affixed to the end and let Alcee play a game of tug-of-war. Then she relinquished the toy and put the dog in a down-stay. They'd both remain out of the way of those working to free whoever was trapped.

The helicopter Erin had heard earlier passed overhead. She'd been right. Bold letters on the belly proclaimed it belonged to one of the local stations. It turned and made several slow passes. If they were looking for a story, they'd found one.

For the next half hour the workers used the crane to remove rafters, beams and joists from the pile, careful not to disturb the stability and cause further collapse. It was like a giant game of Pick-Up Sticks. Erin fought the urge to chew her nails, a habit she'd broken years ago but was tempted to start back up.

The simulations she and Alcee had done at the training facility near LA didn't include removal. Watching the men's painstaking work, praying they didn't disturb a board that would cause the pile to come crashing down, was nerve-racking.

A news van turned onto Boca Vista and drew to a stop. Two people hopped out, a man with a video camera and a woman with a microphone. Erin stepped into the shade of a mango tree and pressed her back against its trunk. If she took off Alcee's vest, maybe they'd assume she was a curious neighbor and leave her alone.

The reporters gave them a cursory glance, then approached Drummond. Whatever the deputy told them was lost under the noise of the crane truck. When they moved toward her, she turned away and held up a hand. "No camera." The last thing she wanted was to have her face plastered on national TV, for reasons that had nothing to do with shyness.

The woman extended her arm toward her associate, palm down, and he lowered the camera. She offered Erin a warm smile. "What a beautiful dog. I hear she's the one who discovered the victims."

Erin responded in the affirmative, then fielded several questions about search and rescue in general and Alcee in particular. Which was okay. She could talk about her dog forever, as long as there were no cameras. While she conversed with the reporters, Deputy Drummond summoned an ambulance and the men continued to work. Suddenly, one of them bent over and shouted something into the debris. Erin couldn't make out the words over the sound of the equipment.

The rescuer straightened, hands cupped around his mouth. "I can't see anything yet, but we've got someone. He's alive and conscious."

Erin released a breath she hadn't realized she'd been holding. *Thank You, Lord.*

The reporters moved in that direction and the camera clicked back on. Deputy Drummond approached the collapsed building. "Ask if he's alone."

The worker crouched to engage in a brief conversation and then rose. "His grandfather is with him, five or six feet away. He's frantic about the old man. Says he stopped talking to him a few hours ago."

Erin frowned. Two victims, one seriously hurt, maybe even dead.

The EMT who'd driven the ambulance joined the conversation. "Ask him if he's injured."

Several seconds passed with just the rumble of the truck's engine and the whir of the crane before the man straightened again.

"He says he's fine, just get his grandpa out. But it sounds like he's having trouble breathing."

The EMT radioed for an additional team, and the men continued their tedious work, opening a larger path to the victims. The second ambulance arrived, and paramedics readied two stretchers.

Finally, the first of the victims was free. He struggled into an upright position, and the paramedics rushed to assist. When they reached the victim, he waved them away. Erin could guess where the conversation was going. The guy was worried about his grandfather and wanted all the attention focused on him.

Some words passed between him and the paramedics. Whatever they said must have penetrated the guy's panic, because he finally allowed them to help him down.

Once on level ground, he looked up. His gaze locked with hers. Suddenly, the ground wasn't level anymore. Her whole world tilted. His apparently did, too, because he froze midstride. His eyes widened and several emotions skittered across his face.

She took several stumbling steps toward him. Cody Elbourne hadn't been her first love, but he'd been her deepest. Then she'd ended it. With that free spirit she'd inherited from her hippie grandparents and four years of college to look forward to, she'd wanted to keep her options wide-open. So after one magical summer, she'd severed contact, a decision she'd questioned more than once over the past twelve years.

Just before she reached him, she jerked to a stop. Now wasn't the time for a reunion. The man had just been pulled from a collapsed structure, and she had no idea what injuries he had.

He lifted a hand toward her, wincing with the motion. "Erin."

Although he allowed the paramedics to ease him onto the stretcher, he remained in a seated position. His T-shirt was plastered to his skin, muscles outlined beneath as he gripped the edge of the gurney. The light brown hair she remembered as being soft and full of body hung in limp, wet strands. He'd likely had a miserable night, lying trapped while pounding rain seeped in through the debris.

A soft whine drew her attention downward. Alcee looked up at her with a question in her dark eyes. Her dog was used to providing emotional support— easing loneliness, calming fears, even settling Erin down after one of her frequent nightmares. But this was different. Alcee likely sensed something was off but didn't understand what.

Erin placed a reassuring hand on the dog's head, offering a smile to back it up. She was all right. At least, she would be, once she recovered. The problem was, the moment Cody's eyes met hers, her universe had shifted, and it still hadn't realigned. It probably wouldn't for some time.

When she straightened, Cody was watching her. "What are you doing here?"

"Searching for survivors." Of course, he already knew that. "I left California a year ago, settled in Fort Myers."

"Oh."

Just *oh*?

Questions tumbled through her mind. What was he doing here? Had he come back permanently, like she had, or was he just visiting? And why Southwest Florida, where they'd both vacationed and fallen in love so many years ago?

Before she could voice any of those thoughts, one of the paramedics slipped a blood pressure cuff over Cody's arm. Erin moved to the end of the stretcher, well out of their way as they did their assessments. The reporters observed from a distance. They'd probably stay until they got a complete story, which wouldn't be until Cody's pops was free.

She hoped it would be soon. Although Cody cooperated with the paramedics, worry lined his face, and his gaze kept shifting to the crane and the men working on the wreckage.

She lightly touched the back of his hand. "They'll get him out. They're good at what they do."

He gave her a weak smile. "I'm just worried about him. He hasn't said anything for several hours. I'm hoping he's unconscious and not…" His eyes dipped to his lap and his fists clenched. "I won't let these guys take me until I know Pops is all right."

"Your grandfather, is this the one I knew?" If she could keep him talking, it might help him keep his sanity while he waited.

"Yeah."

Of course it would be. All he had was his maternal grandparents. His dad's parents had been as absent in his life as his dad had been. His mom ran a close third.

He tilted his head toward Alcee. "I take it the dog is yours."

"She is." The sides of Erin's mouth lifted. It was an involuntary reaction every time she thought of her sweet German shepherd. "Cody, meet Alcee."

He grinned down at the dog. "I'm pleased to meet you, Alcee, especially since you saved my life." Cody's focus bounced back up to Erin, and his smile faded. "I'd fallen asleep, or maybe passed out, then heard a dog barking somewhere above me."

"That was Alcee." Erin patted the dog's back, then pressed the furry body against her leg in a one-armed hug. Almost an hour had passed, but the love and pride she'd felt when Alcee alerted hadn't lessened one iota. "The authorities called us out to see if anyone was trapped."

She resisted the temptation to add *even though everyone was supposed to evacuate*. The best thing Cody could have done for his grandfather was gotten him to safety. If anything happened to the older man because of Cody's carelessness, he'd carry that burden the rest of his life. She wouldn't wish that on anybody. She knew about regrets.

Cody shook his head. "For a while, I didn't think either

of us was going to make it. With those gas tanks blowing, I was afraid the whole place was going to catch fire."

"Gas tanks?" Deputy Drummond stepped closer, brow creased. "There aren't any gas tanks. The heating and appliances are electric."

Cody's face mirrored Drummond's look of confusion. "But there were explosions, about five or six of them close together. Then groans and creaks and finally the pop of splitting wood. The floor tilted, and bits of plaster rained down. Next, the building collapsed."

The deputy's lips pressed together in a frown. He unclipped his radio from his shirt and called Dispatch. "We need an investigator from the Bureau of Fire, Arson and Explosives. One of the victims reported hearing explosions just before the house came down."

Erin shifted her gaze to the home next door. A couple of shutters were gone and a piece of fascia was dangling from the front porch. The roof had taken a hit, too, with patches a shade or two darker where shingles were missing. The home on the other side was in the same condition.

The contrast between those houses and the one where she was standing was startling. Until a few minutes ago, it hadn't made sense.

But maybe there was a reason only one home out of hundreds had been destroyed. Maybe Mother Nature wasn't to blame. Or maybe she'd had some help.

But why? Had someone set out to simply demolish the house?

Or had they been after the people inside?

Cody drifted on the edge of consciousness. Something nagged at him, but trying to analyze what it was required too much effort. Where was he? He wasn't at home. The sounds and scents around him were foreign. But he didn't have the will to decipher those, either.

Awareness advanced, and with it, pain. Everything hurt. The worst of it was confined to his torso. And his head. Yeah, definitely his head.

His chest, too. No, his heart, as if someone had squeezed, shredded, then stomped on it. Pops was gone. It couldn't be true. But the grief pressing down on him said it was. Cody opened his eyes with a groan.

A nurse stood with his back to him, facing the rolling bedside table. He spun and met Cody's gaze for the briefest moment before stepping toward the back wall.

The man had brought lunch. A plate sat in the middle of a tray, a plastic cover hiding whatever was beneath. A packet holding a napkin and silverware lay to the side, along with a beverage. The lights were off, the natural light struggling in through the narrow window offering the only illumination in the room. On such a gray, dreary day, even that was minimal. But the shadows were fitting. Anything else would seem out of place, disrespectful to the memory of the man who had raised him.

Sometime this evening, Erin would return. She'd promised to check on him when she finished her day. At the thought, his spirits lifted just a little. She was the only person in the entire state who understood what Pops had meant to him.

Cody craned his neck backward to check out his visitor. Latex gloves covered his hands, but he wasn't wearing a nurse's uniform. With pants in a nondescript blue-gray color and a button-up shirt in a tiny plaid pattern, he was probably maintenance. His beard was neatly trimmed, and wavy blond hair flowed from beneath a baseball cap, almost touching his shoulders. Was a ball cap approved hospital working attire? More likely in maintenance than nursing.

The man fiddled with something on the wall, then hurried away, hitting the switch on his way out. The room brightened. Maybe someone had reported a problem with the lighting. The guy they'd sent wasn't very personable. But Cody wasn't in a talkative mood.

Pops had made it as far as the operating room, then died in surgery. Ruptured spleen. He'd spent four years in a Vietnamese POW camp, followed by dangerous military missions in places he couldn't even talk about because the US was supposedly never there. And a hurricane took him out.

Footsteps sounded in the hallway, growing closer. Between the solid, rhythmic footfalls was another sound he tried to place, the more rapid click of something against the vinyl tile.

Erin stepped into the room holding a leash. Alcee walked next to her, toenails making little scrapes against the floor. Cody's heart rolled over and his chest clenched. He really needed a hug. He squelched the irrational thought as quickly as it had come.

Erin cast a glance toward the doorway. "Who just left your room?"

"Hospital maintenance. I guess I had some lighting issues. Why?"

"Alcee growled when he passed."

"Maybe he reminds her of someone she doesn't like."

"Maybe."

She stopped next to his bed, and the dog burrowed

her nose under his hand. He obviously wasn't on the people-she-didn't-like list.

He scratched her head and neck. She still wore her vest, its block lettering clearly labeling her a service dog. "So the Dynamic Duo is finished with all its rescue missions?"

"Yeah. We did a couple of searches farther north, where the storm made landfall, but both buildings were empty. We just came from there."

She looked the same as she had that morning—khaki pants and the blue Peace River K-9 Search and Rescue T-shirt, her hair woven into a thick braid that went two-thirds of the way down her back. It had been long when he'd known her before, too. Now it was several shades darker than her natural medium shade of brown, and she'd added a deep auburn-colored tint. It looked good on her. Actually, everything about her looked good.

She pulled up a chair and commanded Alcee to lie down. The dog complied immediately. After her performance this morning, he didn't expect any different.

Erin gave him a tentative smile. "How are you doing?"

He pressed the button to raise the back of his bed. The pain through his torso stole his breath. Though he tried not to show it, her wince said she noticed.

"I'm okay, all things considered." He released the button and drew in a shallow breath. "Three broken ribs, several bruised ones and a doozy of a headache."

"You have a concussion?"

"Probably. They did a brain scan."

"Find anything?"

He grinned. "I do have one."

She returned his smile. "A healthy one?"

"There's a little swelling. I got knocked half-silly with a joist from the second floor, then hit my head on the coffee table on the way down."

She winced. "Ow. Double whammy."

"I'm pretty sure the broken ribs are from that same joist. After clunking me in the head, it landed on my side and kept me pinned until you guys arrived."

"What are they doing about the head injury?"

"Keeping an eye on me. At this point they don't think I'll need surgery."

"Good. And your grandfather?"

Her presence had chased away some of his grief. Now it pounced on him with a fresh vengeance. "He didn't make it. Ruptured spleen."

She cupped her hand over his and squeezed. "I'm sorry." The sadness in her eyes underscored the heaviness in her tone.

The teenage Erin had been all about fun and didn't have a serious bone in her body. At the time, she'd been just what he'd needed. With a dad who'd deserted him before he started kindergarten and a mom whose popping in and out of his life had done more harm than good, that carefree abandon had drawn him to her like metal shavings to a magnet. Of course, that same carefree abandon was the trait that had kept her from continuing their relationship beyond that one blissful summer.

But the way she was looking at him, her hand warm over his, the intervening years must have changed her. She'd matured. There was a seriousness that seemed to now be an intrinsic part of her personality, as if she'd learned the hard way that life wasn't all fun and games.

"It's my fault he's gone." He swallowed hard under the pressure of the guilt bearing down on him.

She squeezed his hand. "Hindsight's always twenty-twenty. Don't beat yourself up. People who haven't been through a hurricane don't realize how deadly they can be."

"I knew. I've lived here in Cape Coral for the past eight years." He'd gotten sick of the Chicago cold and left Gram and Pops for the warmer climate.

He'd had a reason for choosing the Charlotte Harbor area. He'd met Erin in nearby Punta Gorda after his high school graduation when their grandparents stayed in the same RV park. Upon arriving eight years ago, he'd searched for her on social media and even checked parks in the area to see if her grandparents had come back. They hadn't. So he'd closed the door on that season of his life.

Erin had said if it was meant to be, their paths would cross again. They had now, and he was still reeling. He'd thought of little else since the moment he'd looked up and seen her standing there with her dog. At one time it would have been a dream come true, but eight years and one ex-wife later, those doors had closed. Erin wasn't the only one whose life experiences had changed her.

He reined in his thoughts. "What I didn't count on was Pops's stubbornness. He was supposed to be waiting out the storm at a friend's house thirty miles inland. I didn't find out he'd decided to stay in his apartment until we were already catching the outer bands. I went there, planning to bring him home with me."

"I take it that didn't work."

"Not at all. The more I prodded him, the more he dug

in his heels. You might remember Pops had a stubborn streak the size of the Mississippi River."

She gave him a sympathetic smile. "I do. But I also remember how much he loved you and your grand-mother."

"He did." Cody hadn't always known it growing up. Pops had been stern and gruff through those years, a strong disciplinarian. Whether that sternness was in-nate or due to his experiences in the military, Cody wasn't sure. But with his own anger and rebelliousness, he'd needed a lot of tough love, and Pops had provided it, something Cody hadn't appreciated until he was al-most grown.

He shook his head. "I wasn't about to leave him alone. So I stayed." He heaved a sigh, inducing a wince. "I'm the reason Pops was here. When Gram died last year, he took it hard. I couldn't stand the thought of him up there by himself. He finally gave in and moved two months ago. If I'd left him in Chicago, he'd still be alive."

Before Erin had a chance to respond, a sheriff's de-tective walked into the room. Alcee rose, tail wagging, and Erin greeted him by name.

He returned the greeting. "So this is your dog. I heard you two were on site first thing this morning. Good work. But it looks like someone other than Mother Nature might have been involved. We've already started an investigation. You'll be working it, too."

Cody looked from the detective to Erin. What would search and rescue have to do with investigating the ex-plosions he'd heard?

The detective nodded in his direction. "I'm Detective Manuel Gonzales. I see you've already met Detective Jeffries."

"Detective?" Granted, he'd just suffered a head injury, but things weren't adding up. "I thought you worked for Peace River something-or-other, with dogs."

She smiled. "I do. One dog, anyway. But that's on a volunteer basis. My work with Lee County Sheriff's Department is what pays the bills."

Detective Gonzales circled around to the other side of the bed. "Do you feel up to answering a few questions?"

"Sure." He'd had better days, but nothing was keeping him from talking. Other than the pain that stabbed through his side with every breath.

The detective pulled up a chair and removed a small, spiral-bound notepad from his pocket. "The Bureau of Fire, Arson and Explosives is still early in its investigation, but there's evidence of charges being set."

"Charges?"

"Explosives. C-4, dynamite."

Yeah, he knew what the man meant. He was just having a hard time accepting that what killed his grandfather might have been intentional.

Erin was apparently having the same problem. "Why would someone bring down the building, especially with people inside?"

Cody's mind spun. "Maybe there wasn't supposed to be anyone there. Pops's car was in the shop, having some mechanical work done. His friend's daughter was supposed to pick him up, and they were going to head to her dad's house. Then I found out Pops had changed his mind, and I went right over to get him.

When I pulled up, the last resident was leaving. The place looked abandoned."

The detective frowned. "You saw someone leaving the building?"

"I even talked to him. He asked if I was staying, and I told him I was there to pick up my grandfather. The guy wasn't from around here. He had a heavy Northeast accent, like New York or Boston."

"Can you describe him?"

"Stocky build. About two inches shorter than I am."

"And you are?"

"Six foot even."

He paused to jot down the information. "What else?"

"He was wearing a yellow rain slicker. Sunglasses, too, which was odd. We were getting hit by one of the outer bands, so it was raining pretty hard. The slicker's hood was pulled up, leaving the guy's features in shadow, but I could see he had some facial hair. Whether a full beard or a goatee, I couldn't tell."

"Color?"

"Light brown, dark blond."

"What kind of vehicle?"

"None. He left on foot, headed toward Main."

"If you saw him again, do you think you could identify him?"

"It's doubtful."

After a couple more questions Cody couldn't answer, the detective stood with instructions to call if he remembered anything else. He'd almost reached the door when Cody stopped him.

"Wait. There were sandbags."

The detective turned. "Pardon me?"

"When I got to my grandfather's place, I noticed

sandbags. But they didn't seem to serve any purpose, just one or two resting against the pilings underneath the house, instead of stacked to form a barrier." The structure had been constructed like a lot of them close to the water, built to accommodate a storm surge without flooding, as long as the surge wasn't too bad. The arrangement of the sandbags had looked odd at the time. Now it seemed sinister.

The detective made some more notes. "Maybe they weren't there to protect the house. Maybe they were hiding what would destroy it."

After Gonzales left, Erin eyed the tray on the table next to her. "Have you eaten?"

"No. They brought it while I was asleep, and you got here right after I woke up."

"Don't let me keep you from your lunch."

"I'm not hungry."

"You need to eat." She smiled. "Even though it's hospital food."

He wrinkled his nose. "Cold hospital food."

"The covers help keep the food warm. This one's on crooked, though. Did you already check it out?"

"I haven't touched it."

But maybe he'd take a few bites, just to make her happy. He removed the cover and looked at the grilled cheese sandwich. It was cut in half on a diagonal, the pieces angled with a disposable bowl in the space, likely holding soup.

He took a bite of the sandwich. Whatever warmth it had held when it was delivered was long gone. At least it was something that didn't taste bad cold. He finished one of the triangular-shaped halves.

Maybe the soup had held its heat better. He peeled

off the plastic lid and tore open the silverware packet. Alcee rose, sniffing the air. When he put the spoon into the soup, she released a sharp bark.

Erin ran a hand down the dog's back. "What's wrong, girl?"

"Maybe she's hungry." He moved the chunks around with his spoon. "Looks like vegetable beef. I'll give her some of the meat if it's okay with you."

Erin frowned. "She's not hungry. I fed her right before coming up here." Her eyebrows were drawn together, and her face registered equal parts confusion and concern.

"Hey, I don't mind. If not for her, I'd probably still be buried in rubble, soaking wet and half-starved. Instead, I'm lying here in a nice dry hospital gown, enjoying a cold cheese sandwich and a lukewarm bowl of soup."

He scooped up a spoonful and brought it toward his mouth. Alcee erupted in a frenzy of barking.

"Wait." Erin's hand shot out and gripped his arm.

"What?"

"Don't eat that." Her eyes were wide with panic. "Something's wrong with it."

He lowered the spoon. "Are you telling me your dog sniffs out trapped people *and* tainted food?"

"It's possible. She started training as a guide dog, then was changed to detection. She was too energetic for both of those careers and finally landed with search and rescue. Whatever she alerts to, I trust her one hundred percent."

"Do you really think somebody poisoned my food?" No offense to her dog, but the idea was too far-fetched to take seriously.

"I don't know. But Alcee thinks something's wrong, and she doesn't act like this without good reason."

He put the spoon back into the bowl and lowered his hand to his lap. A sense of uneasiness settled in his stomach, that hollow-gut feeling that came when something bad was lurking right around the corner. "But I don't have any enemies."

"Someone just brought down a building with you inside."

"That wasn't aimed at me."

"Look, Alcee is smart. Shortly after I got her, she alerted me to a gas leak. She feels something is wrong with your soup, so we're taking it seriously."

She pressed the call button for the nurse and snagged a pair of latex gloves from a box on the wall. After putting them on, she snapped the plastic lid back onto the soup container.

A nurse entered the room and approached the bed. "Can I get you something?"

"Yes." It was Erin who answered. "We need two sterile, sealable plastic bags."

The young woman raised her eyebrows but didn't question the unusual request. Erin's commanding tone discouraged any argument. After a moment's hesitation, she nodded and left the room.

Erin scanned their surroundings.

"What are you looking for?"

"Anything that might reveal your identity."

Cody did his own search. A dry-erase board hung on the opposite wall, his doctors' and nurses' names written on it. But as far as he could tell, his patient chart wasn't in the room. That information probably came in and out on the tablets carried by the medical personnel.

Erin eased back into her chair. "What about your wallet and phone?"

"Everything's in a plastic bag in that bottom drawer, along with the clothes I was wearing when they brought me in."

Erin pulled her phone from her purse. "We're getting Detective Gonzales back out since I'm not on tonight." She tilted her head toward the soup. "This is going in for prints and the soup for a toxicology workup. And you're having around-the-clock police protection until you get out of here."

He lifted his brows. For someone who'd waltzed back into his life just that day, she was being awfully bossy. But he didn't have the gumption to argue. The events of the past twenty-four hours had him pretty shaken up. "And if the report comes back clean?"

"Then we were extra cautious for nothing. I'll choose safe over sorry any day."

She placed the call, then put her phone away. "I don't know what's going on, who set those charges or why."

Her gaze locked on his with an intensity that wouldn't let him look away. "But I do know this. If that soup is found to be tainted in any way, for you, this threat just got personal."

TWO

Erin pushed a wheelchair toward one of the elevators in Cape Coral Hospital, the rubber soles of her boots making muffled taps against the vinyl tile. She'd gotten permission to pick Cody up from the hospital, take him to retrieve his truck, then escort him home. It was her responsibility to make sure he wasn't followed.

"I'm glad to be getting out of here." He shifted in the chair. "Another day and I'd have been climbing the walls."

He'd been scheduled to be released yesterday, but the doctor had held him one more day, wanting to make sure there weren't any complications. Two and a half days in the hospital had stretched his patience. He obviously didn't do well with confinement.

"So where is Alcee?" Cody angled a glance over one shoulder, but couldn't twist enough to make eye contact. He winced, then released a pent-up breath, gaze straight ahead again.

He'd be sore for a while. Besides the cracked ribs, nasty bruises marked both arms. With the bedsheets pulled up past his waist and the hospital gown above that, those were the only ones she'd been able to see, but she was sure there were others. Considering what he'd been through, he was blessed to have fared as well as he had.

"Alcee's with my neighbor. She keeps her while I'm working."

"You're on duty now?"

"Yep. My job is to make sure you get home safely." A marked unit would respond to secure the area, then follow them to Cody's.

The crime scene techs hadn't lifted any viable prints from the soup container, which didn't come as a surprise since the guy had worn latex gloves. The food service people likely had, too. And the toxicology report wouldn't be back for several weeks.

Hospital surveillance tapes weren't any help, either. The cameras had captured the supposed maintenance person, but he'd managed to keep his head down in all the footage. Though his face wasn't identifiable, hospital personnel were able to verify he wasn't one of their employees, which made his presence suspicious.

She stopped in front of the bank of elevators and pressed the down button. If it was up to her, Cody wouldn't even go home. "What if he knows where you live?"

"Then he'd have waited to attack me when I'm there alone rather than in a hospital ward with people all around. He doesn't know who I am or where I live."

"Unless he looked at your wallet."

"He didn't get that far. He was still standing at my food tray when I woke up. I think I startled him, and that's why he didn't get the cover back over my food properly." He attempted another backward glance.

"That's assuming he tried to poison me. I'm still not convinced."

The elevator dinged, and she shook her head. He was either way too trusting or liked to live in denial. Or maybe it was just plain stubbornness. He'd accused his grandfather of having a healthy dose of the trait, but he'd inherited some of it himself.

The elevator doors opened. An elderly couple and a woman with a teenager stood inside. They stepped to the edge to make room for the wheelchair, and Erin rolled it forward.

A short time later she wheeled him through the automatic glass entry doors. A midafternoon thunderstorm had passed through earlier, and walking out of the air-conditioned comfort of the hospital was like stepping into a sauna. Florida wouldn't offer any relief from the heat and humidity for at least another month or two.

She turned to follow the wide walkway to her right. The main entrance was tucked into the V where two wings joined, a large circular drive in front. Inside the circle several palms rose above a floor of neatly trimmed shrubs. Her county-assigned Ford Explorer waited up ahead. She'd pulled it through a short time earlier and parked at the curb.

After Cody was situated in the vehicle, she returned the wheelchair. He turned to her as soon as she slid into the driver's seat.

"When we get to Pops's place, I need a few minutes. I want to retrieve some of his things. I also need to stop at the bank on the way home. I finished a remodel job the day before the storm, and the customer made his last payment in cash. I have an envelope with almost two thousand dollars locked in my glove box."

She frowned at him. "I don't know about the bank, but hanging out at your grandfather's place is out of the question."

The Bureau had finished collecting its evidence yesterday. The construction workers had even made a somewhat clear path to what had been Cody's grandfather's apartment. It had been the only way to get them both safely out. But the fact remained that there was a killer out there somewhere. And whether Cody was willing to admit it or not, he was a target.

"You said they're clearing the area before we arrive, making sure no one's waiting for me."

"That's beside the point. We're not going to let you dally there."

"All I need is ten minutes. There are keepsakes I don't want to lose, memorabilia from Pops's years in the military, letters, photos."

She cranked the car, then wound her way past the series of medical buildings and doctors' offices to come out on Thirteenth Court. "Whatever is there, it's not worth your life." She sighed. Judging from the stubbornness on his face, she was wasting her breath. But she continued anyway. "Somebody brought a building down with you inside."

"And no one believes that was aimed at me."

"Someone just tried to poison you."

"We don't know that. Not until the toxicology report comes back. You trust your dog one hundred percent. I'm more of a show-me kind of guy."

She shook her head as she eased to a stop at a traffic light. Soon they'd be headed toward Pine Island, where his grandfather had lost his life and where Cody could well have joined him. And Cody was going to remain in denial until he had irrefutable proof.

"What about the man in your room? Law enforcement thinks you're in danger, or they wouldn't have posted a Cape Coral police officer in the hall." She heaved a sigh. He was a lot more exasperating than he'd been when she'd known him earlier. "If the man didn't intend you any harm, what was he doing there?"

Some of the stubbornness fled his features. She didn't give him a chance to regroup.

"We've made contact with the apartment owner and two of the tenants. The others haven't returned yet. But based on preliminary interviews, out of the six apartments, your grandfather lived in one, and one was vacant. The other four were occupied by a single mom with two kids, two middle-aged sisters, a retired couple and two guys. The man you saw isn't a resident there."

"What about the two guys?"

"Tall and lanky, not the build of the guy you saw leaving."

The light changed, and she stepped on the gas. When she glanced over at Cody, a muscle worked in the side of his jaw as if he was clenching and unclenching his teeth.

Finally, he shook his head. "How did he find me? Let's assume the guy I saw leaving set the charges. He wouldn't have known Pops and I were inside when the building collapsed. I told him we were both leaving."

"The story hit the news. Your names were withheld, pending notification of your grandfather's next of kin, but everyone in Lee County knows there was one rescue and one fatality."

She made a left onto Pine Island Road. "Or maybe

he came back to survey his work and witnessed the rescue."

It was possible, especially if he'd used binoculars and stayed hidden by foliage. She hadn't been looking for suspicious observers, because there'd been no reason to assume anything sinister. Her focus had been on her dog, then on the men working to free victims. After that, Cody had occupied every thought. He was still unwittingly injecting himself into far too many of them.

"He'd assume you'd be taken to Cape Coral since it's the closest hospital. Dressed in his fake maintenance uniform, he was able to move about freely. The hospital isn't filled to capacity right now, either." Not like during the December to April snowbird season, when Florida's elderly population grew exponentially.

She sighed. The conversation had gotten sidetracked, and he hadn't agreed to get in his truck and go straight home. Now she had less than thirty minutes to tunnel her way through his stubbornness.

"Why don't you specify what you're looking for, and we'll get whoever's in charge of cleanup to keep an eye out for it."

He shook his head, jaw set and eyes hard. "If I don't get the stuff today, it'll be gone. I'm not taking that chance."

"You're putting yourself in unnecessary danger." She clenched the wheel and reined in her emotions. She usually prided herself on keeping her cool. But this wasn't a random witness she was dealing with. It was Cody. And she still cared for him. Always would.

He was silent for several moments. Maybe her arguments were getting through to him. When he finally spoke, his tone was low.

"How are *your* grandparents?" He looked at her hard, gaze boring into her.

"They've settled here in Florida. Mimi had a stroke, but she's doing well, finishing her rehab."

In fact, they were the reason she was in Florida. After almost three decades of traveling, they'd bought a place in a senior mobile home park and put down roots. Two months later her grandfather had had a heart attack. Rather than her parents bringing them back to California, Erin had left her position as a K-9 officer with Sunnyvale Police, paid the penalty to terminate her apartment lease and took off, pulling a small U-Haul trailer behind her RAV4.

The move wasn't quite the sacrifice it appeared to be. She'd wanted to put some distance between herself and her past mistakes and at the same time escape the fallout from her latest relationship fiasco. The fresh start had accomplished the latter. Unfortunately, the nightmares had made the cross-country move with her.

Cody nodded. "I'm glad you still have your grandparents."

His words were sincere, but she could read the meaning behind them. She didn't have just her grandparents. She had her parents, too—loving, supportive ones. Based on what Cody had told her, he'd never had a father, and his mother had abandoned him more times than he could count. Now that his gram and pops were gone, whatever he pulled from that wreckage might be all he had left of his family.

He'd lost enough. She wouldn't make him give that up, too.

She heaved a sigh. "Ten minutes. And I'll be timing you."

"Not a problem. I'm in no shape to be doing anything too major. I know where the boxes are, because I helped him move. With all the clearing those guys did getting to Pops, it won't take me long to find what I'm looking for."

The other unit would wait, and although her supervisor wouldn't be any happier with the situation than she was, he'd expect her to do exactly what she was doing. If she forced Cody to go right home, she wouldn't put it past him to head back over as soon as she left.

When she reached Pine Island, there wasn't much more activity than there'd been two days ago. Her electricity in Fort Myers had come back on that morning, but power hadn't been restored here yet. Some of the residents were likely staying away rather than enduring the heat and humidity without air-conditioning. She couldn't blame them. Last night had been pretty miserable.

Eventually, the road curved. To her right, three boats bobbed in a light chop, their occupants fishing. Docks extended out over the water, signs on their ends declaring them private. To her left, a vehicle sat in one driveway, but the other homes were still abandoned. A marked unit waited at the edge of Main, the same place Joe had occupied when she'd spoken to him Sunday. Another one sat in front of the demolished apartment building. No one had followed them. Erin had been checking her mirrors from the time they left the hospital.

After stopping next to the white Ram, she stepped from the vehicle, eyeing the caution tape cordoning off what remained of the structure. It was there for safety's sake, with the newly added no-trespassing signs to discourage snooping and reduce liability. Two uniformed deputies approached from the properties on either side.

"All clear. We're just going to look at his truck since it sat here unattended for some time."

Erin nodded toward Cody. "He's going to grab a couple of things while you do that."

Cody ducked beneath the tape, then maneuvered his way across the pile of debris. For the next several minutes she shifted her gaze between him and the deputies at his truck. While Cody searched, one man worked on hands and knees, looking behind each wheel, and the other checked beneath the hood.

Finally, Cody straightened, brows drawn together and lips pressed tight. Sweat beaded on his face, likely from pain as much as the Florida heat. The handle of a metal box was clutched in one hand. "This has Pops's keepsakes from his Air Force days." He set it aside and returned to his search.

A couple of minutes later he made his way down with what looked like an armload of photo albums and placed them on the hood of her Explorer. "There are a few of us in the top one."

"Really?" Her heart fluttered. He'd held on to them all these years. At least, his grandparents had.

"I didn't know Pops had them until I was helping him move. We were taking a break, and I flipped through them." He gave her a half smile. "We have Gram to thank. She was the historian of the family."

He stepped toward the destroyed building. "I want to get their letters. Then I'll be ready to go."

She glanced at the cops checking his truck and then down at the albums. "Do you mind if I look?"

"Help yourself."

She picked up the album he'd indicated and turned back the cover. This one was devoted to Cody. The first page held a school picture, "first grade" in neat script below. Others followed, showing his progression in age.

Baby pictures were absent. Those were the years before he came to live with his grandparents. His mother was obviously a poor picture taker. Based on what Cody had told her years ago, she'd been a sorry mother, too.

After several photos of teenage Cody enjoying various activities, she turned the page to find her own face staring back at her. Cody was behind her, bent so his chin rested on her shoulder. He held her in a tight embrace, arms wrapped around her waist. The love in his eyes was obvious, even in a twelve-year-old picture.

She'd been in love, too. She just hadn't been ready to make it exclusive. Too many years of watching her mother give up who she was to accommodate a rigid, demanding man had made her gun-shy.

Erin had thought she could put what she had with Cody on hold and have the option of returning to it at a later date, both of them unchanged. As if love was something that could be stored on a shelf, then taken down sometime in the future, dusted off and revived. Life didn't work that way. Over the past twelve years a lot of water had gone under the bridge, and it only flowed in one direction—forward. Never back.

She turned the page. In the next photo she and Cody were huddled together on a porch-type swing, her head tilted toward him, one leg extended. Everything about her, from her pose to her facial expression, shouted *carefree*.

Carefree had been an illusion. In her determination to avoid the constraints that marked her mother's life, she'd picked users and losers. One bad choice had al-most gotten her killed. But sometimes it was the unseen wounds that bled the worst.

Erin glanced up as a red Toyota Tacoma turned onto Boca Vista. She stiffened in alert readiness. But the driver didn't show any interest in what they were doing beyond a brief glance in their direction.

The tension fled her body. The man looked nothing like the guy at the hospital. He was clean-shaven, and his hair was dark and close cut. Probably a neighbor. Someone who belonged here.

Cody made his way toward her with the box he'd retrieved earlier, along with a second one. After plac-ing them on the ground in front of her, he straight-ened, lips pursed and eyebrows drawn together. "I just thought of something Pops said the night of the storm. A couple of days earlier the owner of the building told him he wanted everyone gone. No one was to wait out the storm in their apartment." He frowned. "Maybe it doesn't mean anything. Maybe he didn't want the li-ability if something happened."

Erin finished the thought for him. "Or maybe he planned to have the place destroyed to collect the insur-ance money and didn't want to hurt anyone."

It was possible, even probable. They'd know more after checking out the guy's financial situation. The de-tectives were already on it. That was always the most logical place to start in situations like this.

She glanced at the deputies who were now squatted at the two open doors of the Ram, apparently looking under the dash. "Did you not lock your truck?"

"No. I was getting Pops and leaving right away. After my half-hour fight with him, I forgot about it."

She nodded, thankful the deputies were being so thorough. "Have you thought about funeral arrangements yet?"

"I have an appointment with the funeral home tomorrow. Pops belonged to a church here, so I'll get in touch with his pastor. When everything's over, we'll have his body shipped back to Illinois to be buried with Gram." Sadness filled his eyes. "I'm going to miss him. I can't tell you how often something crosses my mind and I think about telling him. It still doesn't seem real."

Erin's heart twisted. At one time she'd have drawn him into a comforting hug. Instead, she put a hand on his shoulder and gave it a squeeze.

She remembered Cody's grandparents well. She'd even heard several of his grandfather's stories. He'd been tough and crusty, what she'd always imagined an old military vet would be. But when it had come to Cody's grandmother, the man had had a soft spot that Erin had found cute. He'd directed quite a bit of that softness Erin's way, too.

"Let me know when the funeral is. I'd like to come." She wouldn't miss this opportunity to pay her final respects to the man she'd liked and admired as a teenager.

She'd be there for Cody, too, not because she'd broken his heart twelve years earlier, but because he looked grieved. Maybe even a little lost. And it struck a chord in her.

One of the deputies approached wearing a frown. Erin's stomach tightened. "Did you find something?"

"Possibly. It looks like the dash might have been tampered with." He tilted his head toward Cody. "Take a look at this."

They followed the deputy to the truck, and Cody slid

into the driver's seat. "You're right. It's like it's not quite tight. It's hardly even noticeable, but I know my truck."

Erin pursed her lips. "There'd be exterior damage if it was storm related. It sounds like someone might have removed it and didn't get it reinstalled properly."

Cody frowned. "I have a tool kit in the back. If you have some latex gloves, I can open it up and let you guys have a look inside."

His eyebrows drew together and creases of worry formed between. He reached across the truck to check the glove box. After finding it locked, he opened it with the key. An envelope lay inside, along with the owner's manual and some loose sheets of paper beneath.

Tension fled his features. That envelope likely held the two grand he'd mentioned.

After donning the gloves, he went to work on the dash, grimacing with the awkward movements. Soon he had the upper and lower portions removed. "I'm no wiring expert, but I'd say this isn't factory installed."

Erin watched him loop one gloved finger around a small bundle of wires wrapped in black electrical tape. It had been tucked into the left-hand side of the dash, next to the door. Each end disappeared into a connector, attaching it to other wires.

Cody backed away, and one of the deputies stepped forward. "I'm pretty sure I know what we have going on here." He leaned down to look into the long, flat space directly beneath the top of the dash, then pried loose a thin rectangular box. He held it in one gloved hand for everyone to see. "This is a tracking device."

Erin grasped Cody's wrist, an icy wave of dread washing over her. "Someone went to a lot of trouble to be able to find you at any given time. Is your personal information on anything in your truck?"

"Just my registration and insurance information. And it was locked in my glove box."

She released a pent-up breath. At least Cody hadn't made it easy for the creep. But the danger was far from over. In fact, it was just beginning.

"Now do you believe me when I tell you you're in danger, that I'm not just blowing smoke?" He couldn't deny it anymore. He'd have to face the truth and take her warnings seriously. She almost felt vindicated.

But when she looked at his fear-filled eyes and drawn features, whatever satisfaction she might have felt fled. Cody had finally accepted the danger he was in. And it had clearly shaken his foundation.

Cody walked toward his truck, clipboard clutched to his chest. Yesterday Erin had escorted him home, along with two deputies. They'd made sure he wasn't trailed and kept watch while he fed a wad of fifties and twenties into his bank's ATM.

No one had attempted to follow him. Of course, whoever was after him was probably counting on the tracking device to do the job. By now the killer probably knew the device led nowhere except the sheriff's department.

Erin had advised him to lie low. Law enforcement would be driving by his house regularly, looking for suspicious activity, but they couldn't provide him a full-time bodyguard. To be totally safe, that was what he'd need.

Remaining locked away inside his house wasn't an option. While he'd been in the hospital, requests for hurricane damage estimates had poured in. Today he was taking care of the first half dozen. The meetings, note-taking and measuring were tasks he could handle. By the time he had to do any physical work, he hoped to be fully healed.

The house behind him was one he knew well. Six months ago he'd completed a master bath addition. Saturday's storm had sent an oak tree crashing through the middle of it. His customer's brother owned a tree trimming and removal business, so the oak was already gone. And Cody had made arrangements from his hospital bed to have his own guys temporarily secure the opening to prevent further damage.

He climbed into his truck and tore off the top two sheets from the legal pad attached to the clipboard. They held measurements, notes and rough sketches that wouldn't make sense to anyone except him. After sliding them into the folder on the passenger seat, he put another address into the GPS.

The folder beside him was titled *Hurricane Estimates*, but only two of the sheets inside were the completed pink copies of his forms. The rest were pages similar to the ones he'd just added—jobs that were too extensive for spur-of-the-moment pricing.

So far it had been a productive day. Although the Gordons were longtime customers, the other people he'd visited were new. Hurricanes weren't fun, but they were great business boosters for the construction industry.

He wove through North Fort Myers, making his way toward Edison Bridge, which would take him south into Fort Myers. He'd started his day meeting a homeowner on Pine Island. Erin wouldn't have been happy.

But he'd stayed well away from Bokeelia, where his grandfather had lived.

The island itself held four unincorporated towns, with Bokeelia at the far northern tip, Pineland below it, Pine Island Center below that and St. James City at the southernmost tip. If anyone had been watching for him to return to his grandfather's apartment building, they'd have been disappointed since he hadn't gone anywhere near there.

Unless they were keeping an eye on the only bridge on and off the island. But that wasn't the case, either. At least, not that he could see while driving. He'd looked. He had no intention of being reckless.

Now that he was off Pine Island, spotting him wasn't going to be so easy. In a large metropolitan area consisting of three good-size cities, it would be like looking for the proverbial needle in the haystack.

He eased to a stop at a traffic light. Three more estimates in Fort Myers and it would be time to get ready to meet Erin for dinner. He'd lined it up yesterday, after she'd followed him home. All that remained was choosing a restaurant. He was leaning toward his and Pops's favorite place, which also happened to be dog-friendly.

He wasn't sure what an appropriate thank-you for saving his life was, but she'd have turned down anything too extravagant. Of course, she'd turned down dinner at first, too. She was clearly not in the market for a relationship. At least, not with him. Maybe she already had a significant other.

That was fine by him. It had taken a few times of getting the foundation kicked out from under him, but he'd eventually gotten it—a quiet, stable life alone beat the emotional roller coaster he'd found himself on too many times. His mom, then Erin, then his ex-wife. For some reason the women in his life tended to not stick around.

Cody clicked on his right signal and turned onto North Tamiami Trail. Getting Erin to finally agree to dinner had required his assurances it wasn't a date and his insistence that Alcee accompany them. Erin hadn't had a preference. Once she finished her shift, they'd meet at the pet-friendly Blue Dog Grill and enjoy a late dinner on the patio overlooking the canal.

Soon, the wide expanse of the Caloosahatchee River lay ahead, sun sparkling off its surface. The road split into two separate bridges, northbound and southbound, a dual concrete-colored ribbon slicing through the view. He began his ascent in the farthest lane to the left. Past the lunchtime busyness and too early for the evening rush hour, traffic was moderate.

The slope leveled out, and high-rises stabbed the sky in the distance. An abundance of palm trees covered the landscape, creating a floor of green, fronds standing out against the pale facades of the buildings. Fort Myers wasn't called the City of Palms for nothing.

When a vehicle roared up beside him, Cody slanted a glance in that direction. A gold-colored older Camry fell back to match his speed. He looked again, and the driver peered at him through amber-tinted sunglasses, blond hair brushing his shoulders.

Cody's heart leaped into his throat, and he jammed down hard on the brakes. At the same moment the Camry swerved into him.

The crash of metal striking metal reverberated around him, and he fought to maintain control. The space between his truck and the concrete guardrail shrank. His front bumper's left corner impacted with a bone-jarring crash that sent the rear end of the Ram around in an arc.

He clutched the wheel in a steel grip, hoping all four tires stayed on the road. The world spun past him— water and sky, asphalt and oncoming vehicles, more water and sky, then roadway again, taillights in the distance.

When he came out of the spin, the concrete guardrail loomed in front of him. A fraction of a second later the truck jerked to a halt, its hood crushed, steam escaping from beneath. Most of his side window was gone, dime-size pieces of it lying in his lap. An intricate road map of cracks spiderwebbed across the height and width of the windshield.

Cody peeled his shaking hands from the steering wheel one finger at a time. Someone had just tried to kill him. Had the other driver hoped to run him through the guardrail into the Caloosahatchee River some fifty-five feet below? If the barrier had been metal instead of concrete, he'd have succeeded.

Cody hadn't seen the man's eyes, but he'd recognized the hair. The glasses, too. Dark plastic frames with yellow-tinted lenses. They'd looked out of place in the driving prestorm rain. But they hadn't been there to block out the sun's glare. Their purpose had been to impede identification.

Even so, the guy wasn't leaving anything to chance. He was determined to eliminate his only possible witness.

A figure stepped into Cody's peripheral vision, and he turned toward the broken passenger window with a start. The guy was big, close to Cody's age but with an additional thirty pounds of muscle. In the rearview mirror, two vehicles were stopped behind him and another man approached, a phone pressed to his ear.

The large guy held up a hand. "Sorry to scare you. Are you okay?"

"I think so." He wasn't sure. He hadn't had a chance yet to take inventory. His side hurt, but it had been hurting before, along with several other protesting parts of his body.

The other man joined them. He was older, maybe midfifties, and not nearly as large. "I've got 911 on the phone. Do you need an ambulance?"

"No, just police. Tell them to look for an older gold Camry with the driver's side smashed in. Did either of you get a tag number?"

The larger man shook his head. "All I can say is it looked like a temporary tag. I wasn't close enough to read it."

"Me neither. But the police could still put out a BOLO for the car."

The man finished the call and pocketed the phone. Cody released his seat belt. Maybe he should have stood and made sure he could walk before he turned down that ambulance. He pulled the handle and pressed on the door with his shoulder. It didn't budge.

The first guy gave it three hard yanks from outside and finally had it open enough for Cody to squeeze through. After walking back and forth in the emergency lane a few times, he was satisfied. Nothing seemed to hurt any worse than it had before.

He pulled out his phone. Both of the men had agreed to hang around and talk to the police as witnesses. But Cody had another call to make, one he dreaded. Erin would chew him out big-time. But he had to call her.

He was supposed to meet her and Alcee for dinner and had no idea how long he'd be tied up.

Before she'd left his place yesterday, they'd each programmed the other's number into their phones. She had his so she could keep tabs on him, and he had hers so he could call at the first sign of trouble. He hadn't planned for trouble to find him this quickly.

Thirty minutes later the familiar blue Explorer made its way onto the bridge. By then the police had taken statements from the two witnesses and they'd left to go about their day. The wrecker was sitting behind his truck, lights flashing, while the driver worked with the cables.

Erin stopped some distance back, well out of the way of the tow truck and police officer, who was just now leaving. She jumped from the car and walked toward him, gait fast and stiff. Was it concern he saw? Anger?

"Are you all right?"

Now that she was close, he could see it—worry. Her gaze flicked down the length of him and bounced back up to his face. Warmth filled his chest, and he scolded himself. That concern would be there even without their history.

"I'm fine. Someone came into my lane."

Okay, that was sugarcoating it.

"On purpose?"

He sighed. No sense denying it. "I think it was the guy from the hospital."

She frowned. "You shouldn't be out running around. It's not safe."

"I've been doing estimates for hurricane damage."

"Where?"

"North Fort Myers, heading down to Fort Myers."

"Where else?"

He winced. "I started on Pine Island."

She clenched her fists. "What were you thinking?"

"I wasn't joyriding." His volume matched hers. "I've got a business. It's not going to run by itself."

"And who's going to run it if you're dead?"

His shoulders sagged. She was right. But what choice did he have? "Do you know what happens to the construction industry in the wake of a hurricane? There's more work than any of us can handle. We're swamped for months afterward."

"Then lie low for a few weeks. The work will still be there."

"The first step is doing the estimates for the insurance companies. If I don't do the estimates, I won't be the one doing the work. I could lose hundreds of thousands of dollars. I can't recover from that." Two years ago, maybe. But not now. His ex-wife had seen to that.

Frustration burned a path through his chest. "Why is this guy after me, anyway?"

"Because you saw him leaving the day of the storm."

"But I wouldn't be able to identify him. Not with the rain slicker hiding his head and part of his face. Add the sunglasses and, as far as I'm concerned, he could be anybody."

"He doesn't know that, and he's probably not taking any chances."

The wrecker driver approached, a clipboard in one hand. "Do you have a body shop you prefer?"

"No." He'd never had to use one. Other than a minor fender bender the year he turned nineteen, he had a perfect driving record. He hoped this one wouldn't go against him. "I live in Cape Coral."

"Then we'll take it to West Coast Collision on Country Club Boulevard."

"I know where it is." He signed the paperwork and watched the man walk back to his truck.

Erin tilted her head toward the unmarked Lee County vehicle. "Come on and I'll take you home. But I'm still insisting you need to find some other living arrangements, preferably somewhere away from Lee County."

"I'll think about it." Not that it would change anything. He couldn't walk away from his business, regardless of whatever danger he found himself in.

He walked with her toward her SUV. "Do you mind taking me by Enterprise? I need to rent a car. I still have a couple of appointments in Fort Myers. I'll just be late."

"I don't know." Though her gaze held sternness, there was humor behind it. "If you don't have wheels, you'll have to stay home." As she walked toward the vehicle, her smile faded and she grew serious. "We're trying to solve this thing. The arson investigators are handling the explosives end of things, but Lee County is working on your grandfather's homicide."

Cody's step faltered. *Homicide.* The word sounded so cold and unemotional. It was used to describe people on TV—characters on crime shows, strangers in the news.

It didn't belong paired with the most important man in Cody's life.

THREE

Erin's sneakered feet pounded the pavement, and her braid bounced against her back. Friend and neighbor Courtney Blake jogged next to her, and Alcee was on-leash about six feet in front of them. To their right, the sun hadn't yet climbed above the treetops. But the early hour didn't deter the dog. She loved her runs, whatever time Erin could work them in.

Almost a week had passed since Cody's accident, and there hadn't been any more threats. It helped that he was staying well clear of his grandfather's old place. He also wasn't going out alone. Until this was over, one of his guys would accompany him on all of his appointments. The fact he was driving around in a rented car didn't hurt, either. Once he got the Ram back, they'd have more cause for concern. *If* he got the Ram back. According to Cody, the adjusters hadn't determined yet whether it would be repaired or totaled.

Without slowing, Alcee made a sharp right onto the sidewalk that bordered Linhart Avenue. Across the street two blocks ahead, a paved drive led through the sports fields that lay tucked behind Fort Myers High School. The area provided a great place to run, and even though school had started the prior week, they wouldn't have to share the space with any students this early.

Alcee wasn't the only one enjoying herself. Running had been one of Erin's passions for almost a decade. During that time, she'd completed several half marathons and numerous charity races in LA. Now she needed to find some in Florida.

When they reached the back road onto the school grounds, Alcee slowed, waiting for the command to cross Linhart. At this early hour traffic was nonexistent.

"Go."

The dog trotted across the street. As they jogged past the baseball field with its green block wall and Fort Myers logo, Erin turned to her friend. "You doing okay?"

"Fine." She was winded, but she was keeping up.

It hadn't taken Erin long to find a jogging partner. Shortly after she'd moved into her home four months ago, she'd run past Courtney's house several doors down and found her working in her yard. They'd struck up a conversation and instantly hit it off. In the weeks that followed, Erin introduced Courtney to running, and Courtney introduced Erin to Jesus. Erin got the better end of the deal. By far.

Without slowing, Courtney took a swig from the water bottle she kept clipped to her waist. "I saw you guys on the news the other day."

"Yeah." This morning was the first time their schedules had coincided since the storm. Between Cody's grandfather's death and the rest of her caseload, she'd been slammed. "Remember me telling you about my brief romance here the summer after high school?"

"Cody something-or-other." When Erin nodded,

Courtney's eyes widened. "He was the guy who was rescued? I thought he lived up North."

"He moved here eight years ago."

"Wow. You both end up in South Florida, he gets trapped, and you and your dog rescue him. What are the odds?" Courtney shook her head, but a smile curved her lips. "Looks like God might be giving you a second chance."

Erin threw her a doubt-infused glance. "I'm not looking for a second chance, and I doubt Cody is, either."

"Why not?"

"I don't know his reasons. I can just tell he's not."

"And what about yours?"

"You know mine."

"Those reasons don't apply to Cody."

Erin looked at her askance. "How do you know?"

"Everything you've said about him. He sounds like a really nice guy."

"They're all really nice guys at first." Unfortunately for Erin, she'd never grasped how to tell when that niceness was a facade. She was a good cop and liked to think she had a decent business head. Sadly, that wisdom and good judgment didn't always carry over into her personal life.

So she was determined to keep her focus on her job, church, Alcee and running. And try to stick mostly with female friends. Life was a lot safer that way, both physically and emotionally.

Courtney frowned at her pessimism. Relationship woes were one of the things they had in common. After pizza and a sappy movie one Friday night, Courtney had shared hers, and Erin had relayed her own pathetic history. Not all of it. Some things she hadn't told anyone except her immediate family. And the therapist her parents had insisted she see for a brief time.

In spite of what she'd held back, she'd still given Courtney more of her life history than she'd given anyone else. But there was one big difference between them. Courtney trusted God to bring her Mr. Right. Erin trusted God to help her continue to be happy with her single status and not try to change it.

They followed the road's leftward curve. The Edison Stadium entrance stood before them. At the fence that circled it, they turned around to head back the way they'd come.

When they turned from Linhart onto Holly several minutes later, Erin's house stood in the distance. It wasn't impressive. In fact, just the opposite. She'd gotten a great deal on the place because it had needed so much work, inside and out. It was a small two-bedroom, two-bath, concrete-block exterior. Someday she'd have it stuccoed.

When she reached her driveway, Erin said her farewells to her friend. "I'll be in touch." Rather than set hours, her shift times varied depending on what was happening. "We'll shoot for the day after tomorrow."

As Courtney continued down Holly toward her own home, Erin slowed to a walk and made her way up the drive. Her yard was where she'd focused her attention. The hedge of sea grapes separating her property from the one next door had been there when she arrived. So had the oak in front and several palms. But the house's foundation had been bare, the lawn sparse and weed-ridden.

Over the past four months she'd seeded and fertilized, added some robellinis to the palms already there and created circular beds around each of the trees, filled with crotons, bromeliads and ornamental grasses. Ixora lined the house, each shrub a riot of vibrant red blooms.

She loved her yard. Eventually, she'd love her house, too. She just didn't know how to get there. The idea of letting a strange man inside made her break out in a cold sweat. It had even induced a couple of nightmares. That was something she should have considered before buying a fixer-upper.

After unlocking the front door, she walked into the out-of-date interior to shower and get ready for work. She and the other detectives were making progress on Cody's case, but it was slow. They'd talked to Jacob Whitmer, the owner of the apartment building, twice. He'd inherited the house from his parents years ago, then converted it to generate some income. An insurance claim would have offered an even bigger payout. Whitmer had been their prime suspect. Then they'd executed the search warrant yesterday and found several letters that had changed everything.

Turned out Whitmer's claims that the place held too much sentimental value for him to let it go were true. For the past six months Donovan Development had been trying to buy it. Judging from Donovan's follow-up letters, Whitmer hadn't budged, even when the offer went to double the market value.

With no more motive, Whitmer had fallen off the suspect list and Donovan had landed on it. If the man wanted Whitmer's property badly enough to offer an exorbitant price, maybe he'd decided to remove the obstacle by having the building destroyed. Chances were good he had an acquaintance with shoulder-length blond hair and a neatly trimmed beard.

Today she'd stake out his business, and she was taking their only witness with her. She'd already arranged it. The change in plans meant Cody had to reschedule appointments, but he hadn't objected. He was willing to do anything that might bring him a step closer to getting justice for his pops.

Two hours later she sat in her Explorer at the convenience store kitty-corner from Donovan's business. She'd chosen a parking space at the end, next to the trash container, where she wouldn't tie up any of the store's prime parking spots and where no one on the other side of the street was likely to notice her presence. Cody sat in the passenger seat staring through the front windshield at an angle, watching everyone who came and went.

He lowered the binoculars to his lap. "Right build, longish hair, but the wrong color. And no beard. Of course, he could've shaved his beard and dyed his hair, but I can tell you he's definitely not our guy."

Erin nodded. "The guy pulling up while we're here is pretty much a long shot, but I figured we'd give it a try. And if nobody gets to it before I go in tomorrow, I'm going to show the composite you did yesterday to Jacob Whitmer."

He frowned at her. "Don't get your hopes up."

She'd finally conned him into having the sketch done, even though he'd insisted he didn't have enough details to make it worth their while. His brief glance through the Camry's tinted windows hadn't given him anything more than he'd gotten from the other two encounters. After thirty minutes of sketching, the artist had a guy with wavy, shoulder-length blond hair and a beard, information Cody had already provided verbally.

He watched an SUV pull into the parking lot diagonal from where they sat. "What does this Donovan guy look like?"

Erin took her iPad from where she'd laid it on the dash and turned it on. After touching the screen a few times, the About page of Donovan Development's website displayed there. She handed the tablet to him.

Cody shook his head. "Definitely not the guy from the hospital."

"No." She'd already checked out the company's website and its owner. Middle-aged with balding hair and a roundish face, he looked nothing like their suspect.

Two men exited the SUV. Cody ruled them out with one glance through the binoculars, then grinned at her. "Surveillance isn't very exciting, is it?"

"You have no idea."

"I'd rather be demoing a kitchen."

She smiled. "So would I."

His laughter filled the car. "That makes an interesting picture—you in safety glasses, sledgehammer in hand, swinging for all you're worth, debris flying everywhere."

The picture was more than interesting. It was appealing. More so on some days than others. Although for stress relief, running offered the same benefits.

Five minutes after disappearing inside, the two men who'd arrived in the SUV stepped out the single glass door and headed to their vehicle. As they waited to exit the parking lot, a pickup truck pulled in. When the driver got out, Cody picked up the binoculars, then leaned forward, tension radiating from him.

Erin's pulse kicked into high gear. "Our guy?"

"I think so."

She didn't have the advantage of the binoculars, but viewing him from where she sat, she saw two- or three-inch lengths of wavy blond hair curled from an elastic band at the base of his skull. The man brought a cigarette to his mouth and took a long, deep drag. A cloud of smoke curled around his face and head. She shifted her eyes to Cody, gauging his reaction.

He tightened his grip on the binoculars. "Come on. Turn this way, just a little."

As she looked back at the man, he flicked the butt to the side, then pivoted ninety degrees to grind it into the asphalt with the toe of his boot.

"Beard?" She was a little too far away to tell.

"Yeah. It's him. I'm positive. At least as sure as I can get with what I saw of the man."

Erin picked up her radio. "I'm calling for backup." Cody's ID would be enough to warrant bringing him in for questioning and finding out what kind of alibi he had for the night of the storm and the time stamp on the hospital surveillance footage. If he owned an older Camry with damage on the driver's side, that would clinch it.

Cody dropped the binoculars, concern etched into his features. "What if they don't arrive in time?"

"Then we'll follow, let the uniforms make a traffic stop." She wouldn't approach the guy without backup, especially while responsible for Cody. The man was wanted for murder. He probably wouldn't surrender without a fight.

For the next several minutes she sat with her gaze glued to Donovan's front door. They were so close. Within the hour, it could all be over. Cody could have his life back.

She glanced over at him. Once the danger was over, would he want to keep in contact? Would she?

She knew the answer to the last question without even thinking about it. Unless he'd changed a lot in the past twelve years, Cody was like her friend Courtney—one of those gems that didn't come across one's path often. She had no doubt they could continue a friendship, as long as Cody could accept her hang-ups and not push for more than she was able to give.

The glass door across the street opened, and a man stepped out. Cody raised the binoculars. "It's Donovan. I recognize him from the website picture."

Donovan held the door open, and the blond guy joined him on the front stoop, his back to the road while they carried on a conversation. A siren sounded in the distance, and Erin cranked the vehicle. By the time the man turned to head to his truck, their backup wasn't more than a block or two away.

She put the vehicle in Drive and eased toward the road, ready to follow if needed.

When Cody looked through the binoculars again, his eyes widened. "Wait. That's not him."

"What?" Her voice sounded shrill in the confines of the SUV. "Are you sure?"

"Call them off. There's a large scorpion tattoo on the left side of the guy's neck."

As Erin radioed a frantic message to Dispatch, two Punta Gorda police cars came into view. The man with the ponytail opened his driver door, casting a glance at them over his shoulder.

The vehicles slowed, and Erin clamped down on her lower lip. If the real villain was anywhere nearby, the presence of the officers would tip him off.

Suddenly, the lights and sirens died and the cruisers sped on past.

Cody released a heavy sigh. "I couldn't see the tattoo until he turned to walk back to his truck. The guy at the hospital didn't have one."

"Maybe he just got it."

Cody shook his head. "It looked old, even a little faded. A tattoo that size, with that much ink, there'd still be some redness and swelling if it was new."

Erin updated Dispatch. As the two cruisers left the parking lot and continued down the street, she returned to the place she and Cody had waited for the past hour.

Cody put his head in his hands. "I messed up bigtime. From now on, I'd better stick to construction."

She laid a hand on his shoulder and gave him a playful push. "Hey, trust me, you're not the first person to make a mistake like this. It happens all the time."

His cell phone rang, and he looked at her in silent question.

She smiled. "Go ahead. You're not on the clock."

He took his phone from his pocket and swiped the screen. "Hey, Bobby."

For the next several minutes she listened to the one-sided conversation. Based on what she heard, he was making plans to go out, or changing plans, and this Bobby was going to pick him up. It didn't sound like it was work related, which meant it wasn't essential. When Cody ended the call, she was frowning.

He ignored said frown. "I had lunch with a friend scheduled for tomorrow. It's now changed to Friday."

"You shouldn't do it then, either."

"He's picking me up, and we're staying in Fort Myers. Bobby and I do this once or twice a month."

He squeezed her shoulder. "If it's any consolation, he's a cop. The only threat going out with Bobby poses is that for the past year, he's been trying to match me up with one of his fellow patrol officers."

Erin laughed. "Sounds like Joe, one of the guys I know from Lee County. He's been wanting to introduce me to a friend of his ever since I came on board. I figure if I tell him no enough times, he'll get the hint."

"Not if he's like Bobby. Bobby thinks *no* means *ask me later*."

At least she and Cody were on the same page as far as relationships went. That friendship she'd been thinking about earlier was looking more and more feasible.

Cody returned his attention to the business across the street, and she followed his gaze. Traffic there had been pretty sparse and didn't look like it was picking up. They'd maybe give it another hour, get some lunch, then come back this afternoon.

"When are you going to let me make good on that thank-you dinner I promised you and Alcee?"

She looked over at him. He'd already assured her it wasn't a date. There was nothing wrong with dinner out with a friend. "How about tonight, after I finish my shift?"

"You're on."

"Have you decided on a restaurant?"

"I'm thinking about Blue Dog Grill."

She frowned. "That's too close to Pine Island."

"It's on Matlacha."

"Which the bridge to Pine Island goes through."

Cody twisted to face her. "We need a place that's dog friendly."

"I'm sure there are other dog-friendly restaurants in the Cape Coral area."

"Yeah, but I know Blue Dog Grill. Pops and I ate there regularly. I can't take you guys somewhere that I haven't checked out first." He gave her a toothy grin.

She wasn't going to let him sway her with his charm and playfulness. "I'm not going to intentionally put you in danger."

"You'll be armed, right?"

"That's beside the point."

"Look, I won't be in danger. The guy who's after me recognizes my truck, which is still in the shop. And it'll be getting dark by the time we get there." The grin was back. "I'm treating you to dinner. Don't look a gift horse in the mouth."

She sighed. He had some good points. Once he got his truck back, it would be different. In the meantime, maybe she could allow him that little bit of freedom.

"All right." She frowned. "But at the first sign of danger, I *will* say 'I told you so.' And you'll be on restriction until this time next year."

If she had her way, she'd keep him locked inside his house until everyone involved in his grandfather's death was behind bars. But that wasn't an option. All she could do was urge him to be careful and not take any unnecessary chances.

She shook her head. Keeping Cody corralled was turning out to be one of her hardest assignments yet.

Cody backed the rental vehicle from his drive, Erin in the seat next to him.

"I figured you'd have gotten a truck."

He shrugged. "It's only a week or two. By that time

they'll have mine fixed or, if it's not repairable, give me the funds to replace it. Until then, I don't plan to haul around any lumber."

In the meantime, he was enjoying his new set of wheels. They'd given him an Acura TLX. It was nice and sporty, the kind of ride that would impress the ladies. If he was looking for ladies to impress.

As he made his way along Pine Island Road, a series of canals lay to the right. That was pretty typical of the area. The narrow, man-made waterways created waterfront living for the maximum number of residents and offered easy access by boat to Charlotte Harbor and ultimately the Gulf. If Fort Myers was known as the City of Palms, Cape Coral should be the City of Canals.

Cody had his own boat, sitting on its trailer next to his garage. He'd last had it out two weeks ago, when he and Pops had gone fishing. The Starcraft wasn't likely to see water again anytime soon. He'd promised Erin he wouldn't go anywhere alone. Sitting in a boat out in the open, whether he was with someone or not, didn't seem like a smart thing to do.

He looked in his rearview mirror at the dog stretched across his back seat. Hopefully, the car rental company wouldn't have a problem with the occasional canine passenger. Just to be on the safe side, he'd vacuum up any white fur she deposited on the charcoal-gray leather.

Erin sat in the seat next to him. The final rays of sunlight slanted in through the front windshield, lighting her hair with a goldish-red glow. Instead of having it confined in her typical braid, she was wearing it down, flowing around her shoulders like a river of fire. She was gorgeous. Twelve years, and she still had the power to take his breath away.

He shook off the effect. This wasn't a date, and he wasn't going to treat it like one. He'd moved far past any thoughts of trying to resurrect teenage dreams.

"I hope you both brought your appetites. The Blue Dog is known for its fresh seafood. It was Pops's favorite place to eat."

"I'm starved. I fed Alcee when I got home, but that doesn't matter. If she's offered a second meal, she never turns it down."

When Erin and Alcee had arrived, he'd insisted on driving. It was bad enough she'd had to drive herself to his place. He'd never invited a woman to dinner, then not picked her up, date or not.

The road rose, and he navigated the last stretch of bridge before reaching their destination. Ahead of him, the sun sat perched on the horizon, streaks of orange and lavender staining the sky.

Matlacha hadn't changed in decades. Colorful little shops and restaurants lined both sides of the two-lane road. The community had been founded as a fishing village and had maintained that relaxed ambience. It was something Cody loved, a welcome reprieve from the city.

He turned on his signal and waited for a single car to pass before turning left into the Blue Dog's parking area. August was in the middle of the off-season. A few months from now the area would be bustling with activity as the population swelled with tourists and snowbirds enjoying the mild South Florida winter.

As soon as they opened the Acura's doors, tantalizing aromas filled the car. Erin drew in a deep breath, eyes closed. "If I wasn't hungry before, I am now."

She stepped out and clipped a leash to Alcee's collar.

Then the three of them approached the yellow building trimmed in blue and green. Block letters near the door spelled out Blue Dog, a paw print between the two words. The sign hanging from the gable bore the establishment's logo—the dog called Blue inside an oval, the white rubber boots on his front feet a nod to the fishing history of Pine Island and Matlacha.

As they neared the entrance, Cody stopped her. "Wait here with Alcee."

He stepped inside, and the hostess greeted him by name. "I'm so sorry about your grandfather. We were shocked to learn what happened. I hope they catch the guy."

"Me, too." Hers weren't the first condolences he'd received. A few days after the storm the media had released Pops's name, and the news had spread quickly among those who knew him. Given the circumstances, Cody still hadn't been listed by name in any of the reports.

He looked past the hostess into the dining area and the patio beyond. At this late hour several tables were empty. They wouldn't have to wait to be seated.

"I'm with a friend and her dog."

"Bring them around. Teri will meet you on the patio."

Cody walked out the door, then led Erin around the right side of the building, where a sidewalk wove between a metal storage container and the air-conditioning unit. He grinned down at her. "The doggy entrance."

When they stepped onto the patio, their server was already standing at one of the small round tables, two menus in her hand. They both sat. Erin gave Alcee a hand motion, and she positioned herself between their two chairs, head resting on her front paws.

Erin glanced around and nodded her approval. "This is nice."

Cody agreed. Potted plants lined the patio, and triangular pieces of canvas stretched above, strings of white lights accenting the spaces between. Dock line strung from post to post sectioned off the eating area from the canal. Across the water, palm trees rose above the mangroves, their fronds silhouetted against a smoky gray sky. It was a tranquil setting, even romantic, which wasn't necessarily a good thing. The last thing he needed to be thinking about was romance.

After Teri had taken their orders, Erin looked down at the dog lying between them. "This is a treat for Alcee. Though she looks at me with those pleading eyes, I rarely give her table scraps."

Having heard her name, Alcee stood and stared at Erin, head cocked to the side and one ear lifted. Erin leaned over until she was almost nose to nose with her. "Yes, we're talking about you. Cody's determined to spoil you."

Alcee tilted her head in the other direction and released a long *"Arrrrrr."*

"That's right. You're getting dinner number two."

"Arrrrrooo."

Cody grinned. "She's talking to you."

"We have these conversations on a regular basis. I have no idea what she's saying, but she seems to know."

Cody leaned back in his chair. Now that the sun had set, the air had cooled slightly, making the temperature comfortable in spite of the humidity. Two other tables were occupied, the patrons speaking in hushed tones. Other than the occasional words that drifted their way, the night air was silent.

Erin released a long, contented sigh. "This is so peaceful." She rested her chin in her hands. "It's like the crickets are even hesitant to disturb the silence."

"We don't have the crickets like we used to. From what I've been told, some kind of exotic lizard was introduced that pretty well wiped them out."

Erin frowned. "That's sad."

He thought so, too. The cricket songs formed a backdrop for so many of the memories they'd made. Cuddling together on a bench overlooking the canal at the RV park surrounded by palms and mangroves, watching the sun drop below the horizon. Walking hand in hand on the Harborwalk that wound through Laishley Park or just sitting on the swings while his grandfather did early-evening fishing from the pier.

That was where he'd kissed her for the first time, there at Laishley Park, right in front of the palm tree sculpture honoring those who'd experienced Hurricane Charley. Two palm trees, one standing upright, the other bent at a ninety-degree angle by the wind, metal fronds extending straight in line with the trunk. The sculpture held meaning for Erin. She and her grandparents had been there to experience the devastation.

Erin gripped the top of the straw and slowly stirred her tea, spinning the lemon around in lazy circles. Her gaze was fixed on the glass, but the distant look in her eyes said her thoughts were elsewhere.

She spoke without looking up. "I've thought about you over the years, wondered how you were, what you were doing."

"Same here. I even looked for you on social media."

Her eyes met his. "I'm not there."

"So I discovered. You're one of the few millennials in the US that doesn't have a profile somewhere online."

"Safer that way." Her gaze dropped to her lap.

He paused, sensing a story behind those three words, but she didn't elaborate. She would share when she was ready. Maybe. Whatever experiences she'd had over the past twelve years, they'd changed her. She seemed more reserved, less open, hidden behind protective walls that hadn't been there when he'd known her before.

She gave him a half smile. "Did you ever take out a post office box?"

The seemingly odd question wasn't peculiar at all. When their summer had come to an end, he couldn't stand the thought of never seeing her again. So he'd tried to convince her to set a date for them to meet up again after she finished school, just to see if that spark was still there.

Even that had been too much of a commitment. Instead, she'd come up with a different plan. If somewhere down the road, either of them wanted to connect, they'd rent a post office box, put a letter inside and hide the key in a designated place at Laishley Park.

"Never did. But I'll admit, when I got to Florida eight years ago, I climbed up on the base of that sculpture and put my fingers between every one of those sideways fronds."

Even though he hadn't expected to find a key, he'd been disappointed when it hadn't been there. He couldn't bring himself to write a letter, though. It had seemed pointless. Instead, he'd met someone else, another free spirit like Erin, someone who'd even looked a lot like her.

He should have known better. For the past year his

ex-wife had been backpacking across Europe with her
boyfriend, and Cody had thrown himself into work like
there was no tomorrow. At least they'd never had any
kids, so history wasn't repeating itself—there was no
little Cody at home wondering why his mommy didn't
love him enough to stay.

"I thought you'd be married by now."

Erin's words were jarring in a she-just-read-my-mind
kind of way.

"Been there, done that. Didn't work out. What about
you?"

"No husband, past or present."

"No significant other?"

The corner of her mouth ticked up. "Been there, done
that. Didn't work out."

He wasn't surprised. Regardless of the changes he'd
sensed, her aversion to commitment was apparently as
strong as ever.

Their server approached and placed their meals in
front of each of them. Alcee's, she set to the side. The
restaurant folks had already cut the unseasoned chicken
breast into half-inch cubes. The dog rose, nose twitch-
ing, sniffing the air. Her tail swished back and forth.

Cody shook his head. "How does she know she's
getting some?"

"I told you she's smart."

Erin checked the temperature of Alcee's food, then
placed the bowl on the concrete. Throughout the meal,
they kept the conversation light, an unspoken mutual
understanding.

When Teri cleared away their empty dishes and brought
the dessert menu, Erin groaned. "I'm stuffed, but this
brownie bottom pie looks awfully good. I could do half."

"Then we'll take a brownie bottom pie and two spoons."

Teri returned a few minutes later and placed the plate between them. Cody hesitated before picking up his utensil. This probably wasn't what Erin had in mind. He should have asked for two plates. There was something intimate about sharing a single dessert.

But that didn't slow Erin down. In a few minutes the plate was empty except for a few smears of vanilla ice cream and chocolate drizzles.

He laid down his spoon with a satisfied sigh. "I hope Alcee enjoyed her thank-you-for-saving-my-life dinner."

Erin smiled. "We both did."

"And when you solve the case, we'll do a thank-you-for-giving-me-my-life-back dinner."

Her smile broadened. "It's a deal."

He paid the bill and led her toward the parking lot, Alcee prancing ahead of them. When he opened the back door, the dog hopped in and stretched out on the seat. Erin settled into the front, and Cody crossed behind the car. He'd just reached the center of the back bumper when an engine revved behind him and squealing tires snapped his attention toward the other end of the lot.

Twin headlights bore down on him, engine at full throttle. He leaped forward and dived between his vehicle and the next, his right elbow striking the pavement. The pain that shot through his arm and ribs momentarily stole his breath.

When he got back to his feet, Erin had exited and stood facing the street, pistol drawn. The car squealed onto Pine Island Road, its rear end fishtailing. Taillights shrank and disappeared as it sped down the road, headed toward the mainland.

She lowered the weapon and ran toward him, panic in every line of her face. "Are you all right?"

"I think so." He flexed and extended his arm. "I'm sure my elbow's bruised, but it's not broken. And I've got some ribs that are tired of taking a beating. Did you see the car?" As quickly as it had happened, he didn't expect a tag number, but a description might help.

"Older Camry, gold. Since I just saw the passenger's side, I can't vouch for the damage that would have been sustained on the bridge, but I think it's safe to assume it was the same car."

She called the police, and they waited in the Acura for them to arrive. The tasty meal he'd enjoyed sat like lead in his stomach.

"I'm sorry. You were right." He wasn't too proud to admit when he'd messed up. He hadn't just put himself in danger. He'd endangered the lives of both Erin and her dog.

Erin didn't respond. Silence was better than the "I told you so" she'd promised to give him.

He heaved a sigh, frustration coursing through him. "I feel like I'm carrying around a tracking device."

"When he tried to run you off the bridge, he probably followed you from Pine Island."

"But I was watching."

"It's not that easy to spot a tail if traffic is heavy enough and they don't get too close. Maybe he *does* know what kind of vehicle you're driving now. After you wrecked your truck, it was logical you'd show up at one of the car rental businesses. There wouldn't have been that many to check."

"If that's the case, why didn't he just follow me home?"

"You didn't go home. You had appointments. It would've been too obvious if he'd followed you to every stop. He apparently doesn't know where you live, but he's got your connection to Pine Island. There's only one way on and off, and it runs right through Matlacha. With shops lining both sides of the road, do you know how easy it would be to find a spot where he could blend in but still see everyone who came onto the island? That means you need to stay away from here. No argument."

He nodded. It had been more than a decade since anyone had told him where he could and couldn't go.

It didn't matter. From now on, he'd listen to Erin.

FOUR

Erin paced her living room, phone clutched in her hand. Alcee's head moved slowly back and forth, brown eyes tracking Erin as she paced. She'd been trying off and on for the past half hour to call Cody and kept getting his voice mail. Why wasn't he answering his phone?

Last night, hearing the roar of the engine and the squeal of tires had just about put her in cardiac arrest. Cody had barely escaped with his life. He'd dived clear just as the car zoomed past, almost clipping the rear bumper of the Acura.

Whoever was after him wasn't likely to give up until police could apprehend him. Or until Cody was dead.

Now she couldn't get a hold of him and was about three seconds away from making the twenty-minute drive from Fort Myers to Cape Coral to check on him.

She snatched her keys and purse and headed for the door. Before stepping outside, she tried the call one more time. Cody answered on the first ring.

"Where have you been?" She didn't try to soften the accusatory tone. He'd worried her half-sick.

"In the shower. I'm allowed, right?"

"For thirty minutes?"

"Almost. I'm a little sore. Someone keeps trying to kill me."

"Which is why you need to answer your phone."

In the span of silence that followed, a nudge from the rational part of her brain said she was being unreasonable. Unfortunately, her heart wasn't listening.

When Cody spoke again, his tone was teasing. "Do you worry about all your witnesses this much, or am I special?"

"This isn't personal. I'm responsible for your safety. Not officially, but I'd like to keep our only witness alive long enough to catch this guy."

She winced. *Did I just say that?* "I didn't mean that how it sounded."

The truth was, it was very personal. And Cody *was* special. One of a kind. If she could ever let down her guard enough to trust a man, it would be with someone like Cody. But the walls around her heart were too thick, set solidly in place a decade ago and shored up with each year that had passed since.

"It's all right." All teasing was gone. "I'm sorry I scared you. From now on, I'll text you if I'm going to be unreachable."

Why did he have to be so perfect? Her chest clenched, and she was struck with a sudden urge to cry. What was wrong with her?

Nothing was wrong with her. Over the past minute and a half, she'd experienced the full gamut of emotions— from worry to the point of panic, to massive relief. No wonder she was a little off-kilter.

"Thanks." She drew in a stabilizing breath. "How are you feeling?"

"My whole body's sore, but nothing's broken that wasn't already, so I've got a lot to be thankful for. And by the way, thanks for not saying 'I told you so.'"

She smiled. It had required a lot of effort. She'd had to take several deep breaths and clench her fists to keep from wrapping her hands around his throat. But Cody had looked so shaken. Besides, she'd been as upset at herself as she'd been at him. She should never have let him talk her into going to Matlacha.

"I had a nightmare." His words cut into her thoughts. "Do you ever have those dreams where you're trying to run away and your legs won't move?"

"Yeah, all the time."

"I saw headlights, heard the squeal of tires. Unlike what really happened, the car in my dream was far away. I had plenty of time to escape, but my legs were stiff and my feet seemed glued to the pavement. No matter how I tried, I couldn't move more than an inch at a time. I woke up in a cold sweat just as the car hit me."

"That's rough. I hope you don't have any more."

She'd had her fair share. Was still having them. Sometimes they were just rehashed memories. Other times her mind used past terrors to write new scripts. Regardless of where they came from, she awoke with a scream clawing its way up her throat and a dog pawing her chest. Alcee was always there for her, no matter how often the nightmares came.

"What are your plans for the day?" She hoped they didn't involve leaving his house.

"I'm returning phone calls and working on estimates and paperwork this morning. This afternoon I'm going to a customer's house."

"Not alone."

"No. My electrician's coming over, and we're heading there together. It's the only job I still have in progress from before the storm."

She frowned. "I don't like the idea of you going out, especially after what happened last night."

"I went near Pine Island last night. I won't today. I'm not comfortable with the situation, either. But I've got bills—a mortgage, a truck payment. I've got to eat. I can't just not work, and I'm not a big outfit like Donovan Development, with managers and construction superintendents and people I can leave in charge while I disappear for a while. I'm pretty much a one-man show."

She heaved a sigh. She didn't like it, but she understood. If she had to walk away from her job, her measly savings would dwindle to nothing in a hurry.

"Let me know when you're leaving and when you expect to be back." That way she wouldn't be worrying about him as many hours.

"Will do. How about you? What are your plans for the day?"

"Mimi's being released from rehab this morning, so I'm taking her and Opa home to their place in LaBelle and getting them settled in. Then I'm going to see Jacob Whitmer, your grandfather's landlord."

"I hope it's fruitful."

After saying her farewells and leaving Alcee with her neighbor, she headed toward the Fort Myers Rehabilitation and Nursing Center in her RAV4. A half hour later she walked from the facility, both of her grandparents in tow, then stopped next to their vehicle. Opa had stayed the past two months with a widowed friend, so his clothes and personal items were already inside, packed in anticipation of bringing Mimi home.

While Erin loaded her grandmother's walker and suitcase into the back, her grandfather opened the front passenger door and helped Mimi in. The red Cube wasn't a typical ride for folks nearing eighty, but there was nothing typical about her grandparents. Opa with his long hair, usually pulled back in a ponytail, and Mimi in her long, flowing skirts, they were throwbacks from the hippie era, but without the drugs.

Until settling in LaBelle, they'd spent the past thirty years in an RV, ready to take off whenever the whim struck. It was a mystery how the two of them produced a man like her father—methodical and organized, unwilling to take risks unless he could control the outcome.

After her grandfather slid in behind the wheel, Erin met him at the open driver door. "I'll follow you guys." The first stop would be the grocery store. After two months away they had a lot of restocking to do.

Opa nodded. "Thank you, Pumpkin."

Erin smiled at the nickname. No matter how old she got, she'd never outgrow Mimi and Opa's pet names for her.

Erin's childhood had been nothing like Cody's. Never once had she doubted her parents' love for her. Her father was an engineer who ran a tight ship but worked hard to provide a good home. Her mother was a stay-at-home mom who insisted she didn't mind the fact that every step she took had to be cleared with her husband.

As good as her parents were to her, Erin had known since preadolescence that she'd never be happy following in her mother's footsteps. Mama never complained but always seemed like a bird who'd had its wings clipped. Erin's main role models had been her hip, exciting grandparents who epitomized the concept of freedom.

Instead of turning the key, Opa sat for several moments, lips pressed together.

"Opa?"

The word was German, but neither Erin nor her grandparents had German in their ancestry. When Erin was young, *Opa* had been her version of *Grandpa*. The name had stuck.

Mimi leaned forward to talk around him. "Your grandpa's afraid I'm not ready to be on my own."

Erin had the same concerns, just hadn't voiced them. Mimi had progressed well in rehab, the stroke's only effects a slight limp and some unsteadiness. It was the latter that had Erin worried.

"Would you feel better if you spent a few days with me?" *She* certainly would.

Mimi shook her head. "We don't want to intrude."

"It's no bother. You'll have your own space in the mother-in-law suite, but I'll be there if you need help. Consider it a practice run for being on your own."

When she'd bought the house four months ago, it was the attached mother-in-law suite that had sold her on the place. With her parents wrapped up in their lives in California, she'd planned for the possibility that she'd need to care for Mimi and Opa eventually.

The next several moments passed in tense silence. Finally, Mimi gave a sharp nod. "One week max."

Erin closed Opa's door with a sigh of relief. A weight had been lifted from her shoulders. Her grandparents were two of the most important people in her life.

After getting them settled into the mother-in-law suite, she headed out. Her first task would be showing Cody's composite to Whitmer.

When she arrived at the CPA firm, the receptionist led her to the office at the end of the hall. Whitmer stood just inside, arms crossed.

The tightness in his jaw matched the stern pose. "What now? I just talked to one of you guys yesterday."

He hadn't appreciated being their primary suspect. Having police search his home and office probably hadn't gone over well, either.

She pulled the composite from the envelope and handed it to him. "We think this is the man who set the charges that brought your apartment building down. Do you have any idea who he might be?"

The annoyance fled his face. He took the sheet from her and studied it, brow creased. Finally, he looked up.

"I'm sorry. I don't. I wish I could help. I want to catch this guy as badly as you do." He handed the sketch back to her.

"If you think of anything that might help us solve this, please let us know."

"Trust me, I will."

She slid the picture back into the envelope. Something niggled at the back of her mind, bothering her on a subconscious level. She turned toward the door, then spun to face him.

Whitmer had said someone from the department had called him. After the search warrant was executed Monday night, Whitmer had been cleared of suspicion. So who had gotten in touch with him yesterday afternoon?

"Do you remember the name of the person who called you yesterday?"

"Detective Roland."

She drew her eyebrows together. "Are you sure?"

"I'm positive. I have a client by that name, so it's easy to remember."

She shook her head. There wasn't any Detective Roland working for Lee County. Maybe it was someone from the Bureau of Fire, Arson and Explosives.

"What did this Detective Roland want?"

"He wanted David Farnsworth's emergency contact information."

David Farnsworth, Cody's grandfather. A block of ice lodged in her heart. "Who was his emergency contact?"

God, please don't let it be Cody. Anybody but Cody.

"His grandson. Cody Elbourne."

Slivers broke loose and moved through her veins. "What kind of information do you have on him?"

"Name, address, phone number."

"Did you give it to the caller?"

"Of course I did. I'm being cooperative, in spite of the earlier harassment."

Without an explanation, she ran from his office, one hand fishing for her phone.

"Ma'am?" The words trailed her down the hall, but she didn't slow down. When she exploded into the lobby, she almost plowed into the receptionist who'd risen from her desk and was crossing the room, maybe headed to the coffee maker.

Phone in hand, Erin mumbled a "sorry" and hit the door at a full run. She needed to let someone at the department know. Cody needed around-the-clock protection. No, the first call had to go to Cody. She needed to warn him. She hoped it wasn't too late.

Because there was no Detective Roland. Not with Lee County or the Bureau of Fire, Arson and Explosives. There was only a killer determined to eliminate his only witness.

Now he had Cody's name and phone number.
And knew where he lived.

Cody's phone buzzed against the desk in his living
room, notifying him of an incoming message. Leroy, his
electrician, was a block away, waiting at a traffic light.
Cody rose, pocketed his phone and picked up his keys.

He'd spent the morning finishing up estimates, re-
sponding to emails and returning calls. He hadn't even
stepped outside. Erin would be pleased.

But he couldn't stay cooped up forever. Bill and
Candy Hutchinson were waiting. He'd started their job
several days before the storm, a master suite expansion.
He'd gotten it weathertight before the hurricane brought
everything to a screeching halt. His subcontractors were
as overloaded as he was.

The next phase of the project would be getting it
plumbed in and the electrical run. Leroy had a short
block of time this afternoon to squeeze in the appointment. He could read blueprints, but meeting in person
would give Cody the opportunity to introduce Candy
Hutchinson to one of the men who would be tromping
around her home and ensure there were no misunder-
standings.

Cody rolled up a set of blueprints and walked to the
front door with them tucked under his arm. Leroy would
be pulling in at any moment. Normally, Cody would
meet him at the job site. That was no longer an option.

Leroy had understood. So had Dale, the guy he used
for cleanup and miscellaneous things that required a
second set of hands. Over the past week Dale had ac-
companied him to several appointments. Cody had been
surprised at the concern these two rough construction

workers had shown. They hadn't even ribbed him about needing a babysitter.

Before opening the door, Cody peered through the vertical blind slats and glanced around his front yard. Nothing looked amiss. Of course, nothing had looked amiss the other times he'd been attacked, either. His assailant had come out of nowhere.

When he opened the door, Leroy's white Silverado wasn't visible yet around the neighboring houses, but he had to be close. Cody scanned the area again, searching for threats. Clouds had begun to gather on the horizon, working up to a thundershower that would likely reach them before the afternoon was over.

The surrounding driveways sat empty. The neighborhood was typical middle class, with kids in school and most of the parents working at this time of day. A few yards from where he stood, three queen palms rose from a large oval flower bed, aloe and other succulents at their base. Between the narrow trunks, he had an unobstructed view across the street.

Leroy's truck cleared a house a couple of doors down and moved closer. Cody locked the front door, then fiddled with the fob until his thumb rested on the automatic start. Leroy was driving from Fort Myers to Cape Coral. The least Cody could do was provide transportation from here.

Besides, the Acura was a fun ride with all its bells and whistles—remote start and driver assistance systems such as lane keeping and road departure mitigation. It even had heated seats. Not that he'd use them. South Florida's temperatures rarely fell below fifty degrees in the dead of winter.

Before he could step off the porch, his phone rang.

Erin's name stretched across the screen. He brought it to his ear with a smile and "Hey, beautiful" on the tip of his tongue. He'd had so much fun with her last night. It had almost been like old times. At least, until someone had tried to kill him.

He dropped the "beautiful" and kept the "hey."

Erin's breath escaped in a rush, making a hiss in the phone. "You're all right."

"Of course I am." He looked around again, half expecting someone to start shooting. Did she know something he didn't? "Why wouldn't I be?"

"You need to leave." The urgency in her tone sent dread trickling through him. "No, wait. Lock yourself inside."

He shook his head. "Do you want me to leave or stay? I can't do both."

"Are you home?"

"Yes, but I'm heading out now."

"No!"

Cody flinched at the sharpness of the word. Erin's panic was shaking his own confidence. "What's going on?"

"Stay inside. And don't go near the windows. I'm having Cape Coral Police sent right away."

She still hadn't answered his question. "What's going on?"

"He knows where you live."

"Who?" His mouth formed the word, but his mind was already racing ahead to how he was going to deal with this new information. If he had to stop working and go into hiding, he'd lose everything.

She barked an order and a voice responded. She was apparently on her radio with Dispatch. Leroy reached his property line. In another few seconds he'd be in Cody's drive.

"My electrician's here."

Leroy began the turn into his driveway, and Cody pressed the remote start. The parking lights flashed and the horn sounded its clipped tone.

The next moment something hot and powerful slammed into him, and he was airborne, sailing in an arc toward the shrubbery. He landed with a thud in front of it. Pain exploded through his body. His ears felt as if they were stuffed full of cotton, and a high-pitched ring sounded from somewhere inside his head. What had just happened?

He sat up as another sound joined the ring, not as high pitched. It came from somewhere in the distance. When he looked around, Leroy's Silverado was parked in the road. He'd just watched the man pull into his drive. How did his truck get out there?

The ringing in his ears was fading, but the other sound grew louder. It was sirens. Emergency vehicles were in the area. Were they there for him and whatever had just happened?

The Silverado's driver door swung open. Leroy jumped out and ran toward him. "Are you okay?"

Cody cleared his throat, not sure how to answer the question. "What happened? I was getting ready to step down off the porch and…"

He swiveled his head to look in that direction, and his heart lodged in his throat, choking off whatever he'd planned to say. All that was left of the Acura was a burnt-out, mangled hunk of metal.

The sirens grew closer. Beyond the house next door, flashing blue and red lights appeared, probably the result of Erin's call.

He squeezed his eyes shut and moved his head from side to side. Although the ringing in his ears was fading, his brain felt as if it had been slammed around and turned to mush. Someone had just blown up the Acura. No wonder Erin had called to warn him.

Erin! He'd been talking to her when it happened.

He pushed himself onto his hands and knees, and Leroy eased him back down. "Take it easy. You could be hurt."

"I need my phone." Erin would be beside herself.

He scanned the area. The blueprints he'd held lay between him and the porch, the roll bent at an odd angle. His phone had landed beneath one of his viburnum bushes, his keys several feet away.

"My phone's there, under the hedge." Cody pointed toward the house. He couldn't have stood if he'd wanted to. His joints had turned to Jell-O. The broken ribs and other bruises weren't feeling so well, either.

Leroy retrieved the phone, and as he approached, high-pitched shouts poured from it, reaching Cody before Leroy even handed it over. A Cape Coral police cruiser spun into his driveway and screeched to a halt. A second one stopped in the road right behind it.

Cody put the phone to his ear. "Erin?"

A river of words blasted through it, several pitches higher than normal. Actually, a geyser. He didn't understand a single one.

"I'm okay." He struggled to calm his racing heart. "Someone blew up the rental car."

She continued to ramble, sprinkling in an intelligible word here and there—*boom, scared, worried, dead.* Then there was a hitched breath and what sounded like a strangled sob. Was she crying?

Maybe that was what he should be doing. Or praying, thanking God he was still alive. If he did that type of thing. He didn't.

But he should feel something. Scared, relieved, thankful, shaken. Right now he just felt numb.

He tried to gather his scattered thoughts. "The police are here. I need to talk to them."

"I'm headed your way."

"It's okay. I'm not hurt." He didn't want her driving in a panic.

"I'm coming anyway."

That was fine with him. He wanted to see her. In fact, there was no one he wanted more. How much he longed for her should disturb him. Maybe it would. Later. Now the numbness was fading, and horror was setting in.

If that had been his Ram…

He loved his Ram. He'd bought it right after opening his business. It had served him well, but it was a basic model, none of the upgrades the Acura had boasted.

And no remote start.

If he'd had his Ram, he'd have been sitting in the cab when the engine turned over. And he'd be dead right now, pieces of him scattered all over the neighborhood. A shudder pulsed through him. He wished he could just stay numb.

Two police officers approached, and Leroy helped him to his feet.

The younger of the two spoke. "What happened here?"

"Somebody blew up my car."

"I see that." The officer pulled a notepad from the shirt pocket of his black uniform. He looked to be close to Cody's age, possibly a year or two older. But his demeanor was much more relaxed. Maybe exploding vehicles weren't a big deal to him. To Cody, they were, especially when he was supposed to have been inside.

"How about starting from the beginning?"

"I was heading out the door, clicked the remote start on the fob and *boom!*" He paused. "Well, that's not the beginning."

He filled the officer in on everything, starting with arriving at his grandfather's apartment the day of the storm and ending with the events of a few minutes ago. "There's already an ongoing investigation with Lee County."

After jotting down some more notes, the officer turned to Leroy. "Did you see anything?"

"Just the explosion. I was pulling into the driveway when it happened. I threw the truck in Reverse, backed up and parked there." He pointed to where his truck sat in the road, the right tires barely off the pavement.

"I assume neither of you saw anyone suspicious?"

"No." They answered in unison.

Whoever had planted the bomb had probably come during the night while everyone was fast asleep.

Cody swallowed hard. His heart rate was gradually slowing, but it would be a while before the shakiness left his limbs. "Someone from Lee County is on her way, one of the detectives. The Bureau of Fire, Arson and Explosives is involved, too."

The Bureau was going to have more to investigate than the charges that had brought down the apartment building. Whoever was trying to kill him had a disturbing preoccupation with blowing things up.

FIVE

Erin stared up at the red light in front of her, hands clutching the wheel in a white-knuckled grip. Moisture coated her palms, and her right leg trembled, maintaining its pressure on the brake pedal. "Come on. Turn green."

She drew in a stabilizing breath and loosened her grip. Cody had said he was okay. Maybe he was downplaying his injuries. But he wasn't dead. And he wasn't hurt too badly to communicate.

The light changed, and after a quick glance in both directions to make sure no one was infringing on her green, she jammed the gas and roared through the intersection.

Learning the killer knew Cody's whereabouts had sent her pulse into overdrive. Hearing the explosion over the phone had almost put her into cardiac arrest. As the seconds stretched into a minute, then two, she'd believed the worst. And twenty-five minutes away in Fort Myers, there'd been nothing she could do beyond what she'd already done—asking Dispatch to call for help.

She made a right onto Colonial Boulevard and headed for Midpoint Bridge, straight ahead. As she descended a few minutes later, the Welcome to Cape Coral sign greeted her, the Iwo Jima Memorial replica next to it, a variety of flags waving in the background. She'd crossed the Caloosahatchee River and was beyond the halfway point. Soon she'd see Cody with her own eyes and be assured he was okay.

The emotions colliding inside her during the moments between the explosion and Cody's assurances had shaken her. As a law-enforcement officer, her job was to defend and protect the citizens of Lee County. No matter how long she served, she'd never become desensitized to the pain of others. It was what made her human.

But this was different. She'd been near hysteria, unable to bear the thought of losing Cody.

Losing Cody? He wasn't hers to lose. She'd made her choice. If she had it to do over again, that choice would be no different.

When she'd come to Florida a year ago, she'd remembered the deal they'd made. But she hadn't wanted to connect. She'd been afraid what they'd had that summer would no longer be there. And afraid it would be.

Twelve years had passed, but nothing had changed. In the ways that mattered, she was the same girl she'd been then, but with even less likelihood of a relationship in her future. Now she wasn't only commitment phobic, she was commitment phobic with baggage. Just thinking about anything that hinted of "forever" almost made her hyperventilate.

After almost getting killed by an obsessed boyfriend, it had been a long time before she was willing to date again. Gradually, she'd gotten back out there. No one had ever hurt her after that. Not physically, anyway.

After several casual relationships, she'd met someone wonderful and fallen hard. At least, she'd thought he was wonderful…until she'd caught him in bed with her best friend.

Then she'd fallen even harder. Hard enough she'd almost not been able to get back up.

Whatever she felt for Cody, she'd keep it to herself. If she allowed a romantic relationship to develop between them, she'd come to the same conclusion she had before—that no matter how much she loved him, she couldn't do it. Hurting him like that once was enough.

When she turned from Trafalgar onto Twenty-Second Court, she leaned forward. Cody's house stood in the distance. A white Silverado was parked in the street in front, a Cape Coral police cruiser behind it. She roared closer. A second police vehicle sat in the driveway behind the burnt-up rental car. Other than some dents and gouges and charred paint on one of the garage doors, the house looked undamaged.

She screeched to a halt behind the vehicles on the road. Some people had gathered in the front yard, two uniformed police officers and a man dressed in jeans and a polo shirt bearing a logo she couldn't make out. He was probably the electrician Cody had mentioned. Cody stood among them.

As she sprang from the car, the officers turned and moved toward their vehicles, apparently finished with their reports. She swept past them without a second glance. When Cody's eyes met hers, she had to squelch a sudden urge to throw her arms around him and bury her face in his chest.

"Are you the Lee County person Cody said was coming?"

The voice came from behind her. Several seconds passed before the question registered, along with the fact that it was addressed to her. She swiveled her head toward the officer who'd spoken.

"Yes." The truth of that emphasized how inappropriate her actions would've been had she acted on impulse.

After a brief conversation with them, where they filled her in on the latest developments, she approached Cody and the other man. She could see the logo now. Jacobsen Electric.

She gave him a nod and turned to Cody. "You're not safe here. You have to disappear."

"And how am I supposed to support myself while I'm gone?"

She pursed her lips. She didn't have an answer. She couldn't even promise him it was temporary. Some people went into witness protection and remained there for years.

"Then stay with me." The words were out before she thought them through.

"No way. This guy means business. While he's blowing things up, he's not worrying about innocent bystanders. I won't put you in danger."

Jacobsen held up an index finger. "While you guys discuss this, I'll wait in my truck."

Cody nodded at the man. "Thanks, Leroy. We still have to go by the Hutchinsons'. I'll just be a minute."

Erin crossed her arms. He didn't need to be going anywhere except away from Lee County. "Staying here isn't an option. I wouldn't put it past this guy to burn your house down with you inside."

His jaw tightened, and his eyebrows dipped toward

his nose. "Both my house and I would be safer if I was somewhere else."

"What about out-of-state friends?"

"I've got several, but I don't want any of them to support me. I've had my own source of income since I was sixteen."

Yes, he had. When she'd met him, he'd been working for his uncle, a general contractor, on weekends and during summers and school breaks for the prior two years. He'd had a decent car that he'd paid for himself and already had a skill that wasn't related to sports or video games. She'd been impressed.

He wasn't backing down. "I need to be close enough to run my business, meet with customers and assign work to my subcontractors."

"I have an idea." It was feasible. A way to help him and benefit her at the same time. "I bought a fixer-upper four months ago. I'm living with avocado-green countertops and harvest-gold appliances that are older than I am. I'm amazed they still work. I'd planned to have most of the work done by now, but I haven't even started." Now she could get it done without sacrificing her peace of mind.

She held up a hand. "Before you say no, I've got a gun and a dog. And I have a monitored security system. As long as you stay put, no one will know you're there. I'll pick up what you need or have Lowe's or Home Depot deliver it."

There was only one downside—Mimi and Opa. But no one would be looking for Cody in Fort Myers. And with Mimi's independent streak, Erin didn't expect their visit to last much longer than three days.

Cody stood in silence, thoughts churning behind

those brown eyes. Finally, he gave a sharp nod. "All right. I'll cut you a deal. I'd do the work for free in exchange for the place to stay if I didn't have to still pay my bills. Hopefully, by the time I finish your job and am ready to start the next, this will all be over."

Erin expelled a relieved sigh. Cody would be safe, and she'd get her renovations completed without anxiety. At least not the kind that came with the thought of trusting a strange man with access to her haven.

Instead, there'd be the stress of guarding her heart, keeping the walls around it intact enough to be impervious to Cody's charm and good looks and the history between them. But she was an adult. She'd deal.

"All right, then. If you still insist on making that stop you mentioned, you ride with Leroy and I'll follow. I want to make sure you're not tailed."

"I have to get some things together, unless you want to share your toothbrush and deodorant. I also need to grab some tools. Unfortunately, the stuff I used for doing estimates and light work was in a toolbox in the trunk of the Acura."

As she followed him toward the house, a quivery weakness lingered in her limbs. Cody wasn't doing much better. His eyes were haunted, and the color still hadn't returned to his face.

She stepped inside and looked around. She'd been here twice but hadn't gone into the house either time. With its stuccoed exterior and gables in varying sizes, she'd guessed at a modern interior with vaulted ceilings. She'd been right.

"This is nice. Did you build it?"

"I did."

It was an open floor plan, with a large combo living/

dining area. The dining room led to a kitchen that was separated from the living room by an eight-foot-high wall. The ledge on top held a couple of model boats, painted wooden ducks and a series of collector mugs.

A shirt was draped over the arm of the couch, and crumbs lined the plate he'd left sitting on his desk. The empty glass on the coffee table had a coaster under it to protect the wooden surface. The house looked lived in, not overly neat, but not messy, either.

"I'm getting my stuff together, so make yourself at home."

He disappeared down the hall and returned five minutes later wheeling a large suitcase. In the living room, he put his laptop in its bag, along with the power cord and mouse, then pulled a loose-leaf binder from a bookcase. "A portfolio of some of the work I've done. It might give you some ideas." He handed it to her with a grin. "At least it'll help assure you that I know what I'm doing."

He continued to a door off the side of the dining area. "We'll take everything through the garage, since I've got tools to get. Fortunately, I've got extras of all of the small stuff."

She followed him through the door into a well-stocked workshop, equipped with a table saw, lathe, band saw, radial arm saw and a few other items she couldn't identify. Two long racks held wood, and a variety of smaller tools hung from hooks pressed into pegboards.

"Now I see why you park in the driveway even though you have a two-car garage."

He gave her a sheepish smile. "This was supposed to be a temporary arrangement, but it's turned into more than five years. Eventually, I'll build a workshop in the back. Then I'll actually have a garage."

Cody loaded everything he needed for the foreseeable future into her car. "One more thing. I've got stuff in the fridge that's going to be spoiled before I get back. I'd rather not have a laboratory going on in there. Have you got room for a few things?"

"I'll make room."

He disappeared inside, then came out wheeling a large cooler. After putting it in the back of the Explorer, he climbed into the Silverado. When they arrived at the Hutchinson home on the other side of Cape Coral, a man was circling the yard on a riding mower. Erin parked on the road and picked up Cody's portfolio. As she flipped through the pages, she studied each photo for ideas. She'd made a wise choice having Cody tackle her projects. He did beautiful work.

Fifteen minutes later the front door swung open, and Cody and his electrician stepped out. A woman followed, presumably Mrs. Hutchinson. By that time the mower had moved to the back side of the house. Though Erin couldn't see it anymore, she could still hear the rumble of the engine through her open windows.

After a brief three-way conversation on the porch, Cody and his electrician moved down the drive. Leroy got into the Silverado, and Cody continued to her vehicle. When he opened his door, a gust of wind swept through, heavy with the scent of rain.

Erin watched him slide into the passenger seat with a groan. Poor guy. The abuse to his body seemed to never end. She gave him a sympathetic smile. "Anywhere you need to go before my place?"

"Not today."

"Good." Heavy charcoal-colored clouds were piled on the western horizon, rolling closer. A bolt of lightning zigzagged downward. Maybe they'd make it home before the sky opened up, but it was doubtful.

Cody was watching it, too. "Once we figure out meals, I'd like to get a list together and pick up groceries. When you're working, I'm happy to do meal prep. I'm a decent cook."

She grinned over at him. "A jack-of-all-trades."

"I learned out of necessity. After growing up with Gram's cooking, TV dinners got old in a hurry."

He didn't mention the period of time he was married. Was his wife a good cook, or had he cooked for her? Erin shook off the thought. Why was she thinking about his ex-wife, anyway?

Cody pulled out his phone. "I'm letting my neighbor know what's going on. I'll ask him to watch the place, get the mail and so on. He won't mind. I've done the same for him while he's been on vacation."

As she made her turn onto 41, the first fat raindrops hit the windshield. Cody pocketed his phone. A bright flash lit the sky to the right, and a boom followed a second or two later. By the time she began her climb up the Caloosahatchee Bridge, sheets of rain slashed against the car. The Edison Bridge lay a half mile to their left, visible on a clear day. But the summer thunderstorm had reduced visibility to about twenty feet.

She glanced over at Cody. One week had passed since his car accident. They were now one bridge over. But this one was the same height, and they were crossing it in pouring rain. Cody stared straight ahead, gaze fixed on the taillights in front of them. His white-knuckled grip on the door handle betrayed his uneasiness.

Erin turned on her signal and moved into the left lane. A concrete barrier separated them from oncoming traffic. Maybe it would be easier for Cody if they avoided the lane nearest the edge of the bridge. She understood trauma and how it could mess with the psyche, making simple things terrifying. She hoped his experience wouldn't be the cause of too many nightmares.

She knew about those, too. It didn't matter how much time had passed. Some traumas burrowed so deep into the subconscious, digging them out was almost impossible.

Finally, water gave way to land, and Cody relaxed.

She gave him a sympathetic smile. "Sorry I had to put you through that."

He frowned. "I didn't expect it to bother me. As a kid, I had a fear of bridges, but I got over it. I had to, living here. But once you started driving up the incline, with water all around, all I could see was the world spinning, then the concrete barrier in front of me, and I remembered the helplessness I'd felt, wondering if it was going to hold."

"It gets easier with time." At least that was what everyone said.

A while later she turned into her driveway and killed the engine. Her place didn't hold a candle to Cody's, but it was home, and she loved it. Besides, the yard looked great.

But Cody wasn't looking at the house or the yard. His gaze was fixed on the car sitting next to her.

"Is someone here?"

"That's Mimi and Opa's car."

His eyes narrowed. "Why is it here?"

"They're staying with me for a few days. Opa didn't

feel comfortable bringing her back to their home in La-Belle yet."

Cody nailed her with a glare. "And you figured you'd keep this from me until we got here?"

"I wasn't trying to keep anything from you." Well, maybe she was. If she'd mentioned that Mimi and Opa were here, he'd never have agreed to come.

"Take me back home. You talked me into this, against my better judgment, convincing me you can defend yourself. I'm not going to risk bringing this creep down on a couple of old people."

Erin winced, glad Mimi hadn't heard that comment. She'd never considered herself old. Probably never would as long as she was on this side of the grass.

She heaved a sigh. "We'll be in the house, and they'll be in the mother-in-law suite. It's two separate residences." Sort of. There was an adjoining door between, one she intended to leave open, at least unlocked. "Unless you want to go into witness protection or leave the area, this is the only place you'll be safe."

He crossed his arms but didn't argue. Maybe she should have given him a heads-up. She could have mentioned it when they were leaving his customer's house. It wouldn't have made a difference. He wasn't happy. But he was safe. And that was all that mattered.

Cody leaned back in one of Erin's dining room chairs. Alcee had made her rounds, lying next to Erin, then visiting her grandparents and lastly moving to him. They'd been finished with dinner for some time and had spent the past hour catching up.

Erin rose from the table and addressed her grandparents. "You guys take it easy. Cody and I will have this mess cleaned up in no time."

The plates Cody carried to the kitchen were each scraped clean, a testament to how good the food had been. But he hadn't cooked it. At least, not alone. Erin had called in and taken the rest of the day off. While her grandparents had napped, the two of them had whipped up a large dish of lasagna, oven-grilled brussels sprouts and a huge tossed salad. Putting away all the food he'd brought had involved some skilled rearranging, but they'd done it. Now they were all pleasantly full, and the refrigerator was a little less so.

Cody finished clearing the table while Erin filled a sink with soapy water.

"I have a dishwasher, but it doesn't work. Fortunately, my stove and fridge are still limping along. I'm hoping they hang in there till you finish my remodel."

"We'll make the kitchen first on the list."

Cody was anxious to get started. He'd always enjoyed building things. As a kid, it was models—cars, airplanes, boats, spaceships. Then at age sixteen he'd started working part-time with his uncle building houses. Though Gram and Pops had started a college fund for him, after one semester, he'd decided the college track wasn't for him. His passion was working with his hands, his dream to have his own construction company.

Gram and Pops had supported his decision. In fact, they'd always been behind him 100 percent, even when he hadn't been able to see it at the time. The familiar hollow feeling settled in his gut. Spending the past few hours with Erin's grandparents had made him realize how much he missed his own.

He approached the sink to rinse the dishes Erin had washed. As he stood next to her, his chest filled with warmth, a sense of intimacy. It was the same thing he'd felt cooking with her. Years ago he'd been sure they were facing a lifetime of activities, both exciting and mundane, made special simply by the fact they were doing them together.

But feelings changed, and dreams faded. And nothing lasted a lifetime.

He took the towel hanging from the oven handle and dried the dishes he'd rinsed. The large breakfast nook was separated from the kitchen by a bar. On the opposite wall, someone had made several two-foot-long swipes with a roller, each in a different color.

He grinned and nodded in that direction. "Trouble choosing a paint color?"

"Apparently. But that wasn't me. The sellers had started remodeling but didn't get very far. According to the Realtor, they ended up separating right after that. So I got a good deal on the place."

"Tomorrow I'll make some lists and work up prices." Erin had already taken him through the house, portfolio in hand, and given him her vision of what she had in mind for each room. "By the time you get home tomorrow evening, I might have some samples for you to look at." He paused. "Depending on what time I get my truck back."

It was ready. West Coast Collision had called that afternoon to let him know. He'd been surprised to learn a few days ago that the frame wasn't bent, so the truck was repairable. Apparently, the three-sixty he'd done on the bridge had reduced his speed enough that when he'd struck the guardrail, his front bumper had absorbed most of the impact.

But getting the truck wouldn't be that simple. Erin and the others had come up with a plan. Someone in law enforcement would drive it while the others set a trap, keeping watch in unmarked units at various points along the route to see if anyone followed.

She frowned. "Regardless of when you get your truck, you shouldn't go out any more than necessary. Let me bring you what you need and, if you have to do estimates, ride with your guys."

"Fair enough. But Lowe's is a mile away. I've got to pick up things as I need them, or I'll be working on your project till Christmas. Two years from now."

She let the water drain from the sink and put away the dishes he'd dried.

He waited till she'd finished. "Shall we join Opa and Mimi?"

Using Erin's names for her grandparents felt odd. During their whirlwind summer romance, it had been natural. He'd thought they'd eventually be his grandparents, too. When he'd tried *Mrs. Jeffries* this afternoon, Erin's grandmother had objected. They were *Mimi* and *Opa* to Erin, and there was no reason they shouldn't be *Mimi* and *Opa* to him. Apparently, the fact that he and Erin were no longer a couple wasn't a reason.

When he followed Erin into the living room, her grandfather had the TV remote in his hand, scrolling through the options Netflix offered.

He watched them cross the room. "Mimi and I were wondering about watching a movie. What do you think?"

"Sure." Cody and Erin answered in unison.

As the opening credits rolled, Alcee hopped up to crowd into the space between Cody and Erin. Her tail beat against Cody's legs, and her front paws rested in Erin's lap. The tail slowed and stopped, and she eventually laid her head between her paws, eyes closed.

Over the past two months Cody and Pops had watched countless movies together. At least, they'd started them together. Pops had slept through the end of every one. They'd laughed about how Cody always had to tell Pops the ending the following day.

If only he'd known how little time they had left, he'd have made more trips back to Chicago over the past eight years. Or never left to begin with. And he wouldn't have wasted so much of his childhood being at odds with the old man.

Pops had blamed Cody's mother. Every time things would almost return to normal, she'd pop back into their lives with apologies and promises. Both were meaningless, because nothing ever changed. Eventually, Cody would wake up to find her gone, a note lying on the kitchen table.

In the weeks that followed, he'd be mad at the world, ready to pick a fight with anyone who looked at him the wrong way. Finally, Pops had told his mother that if she pulled one more disappearing act, to not bother coming back. Cody had been thirteen and hadn't seen her since. At the time he'd thought he'd never forgive his grandfather. In hindsight, it had been the best thing the old man could have done for him.

When the movie ended two hours later, Opa rose. "We're heading to bed." He helped Mimi up and led her the few steps to her walker.

Erin pressed the power button on the remote, and the screen went dark. "How about leaving the door cracked? I want to be able to hear you if you need anything during the night."

Cody watched them cross the living room toward the mother-in-law suite. Though Mimi had both hands on her walker, Opa walked next to her, an arm draped across her shoulders.

Cody smiled. His grandparents had had the same kind of relationship. Pops had been as tough as could be, stubborn to a fault. Gram had been the sweetest person Cody had ever known, but one stern look from her, and Pops had always caved. She'd even gotten him into church, over his adamant objections. Surprisingly, it had stuck. One of the first things he'd done on arriving in Florida was find services to attend.

After Gram passed, Cody had hoped Pops would find happiness again. But every time a widowed lady had shown interest in him, his response had always been the same—"She's not Gram." Maybe that kind of love happened only once in someone's lifetime.

Would Cody ever find the same thing? He'd thought he had. Twice. And he'd struck out both times. He didn't know how to choose them like Pops and Opa did.

While Erin set the alarm and turned out the lights, Cody headed down the hall in the opposite direction Mimi and Opa had gone. His room was the first one. The middle bedroom was set up as an office, with a desk, bookcases and a daybed. The master bedroom was at the end.

He'd just closed the door when two soft knocks sounded.

"Do you have everything you need?" Erin's voice

came through the door. "Extra pillows? Blankets? I keep the air set pretty low at night."

He glanced at the double bed with its two pillows and what looked like a handmade quilt. "I'll be fine."

He opened the door. "I appreciate everything you're doing for me. You started out the day living alone and ended it with three houseguests. You're good at going with the flow."

"You three are easy guests, not very demanding." The edges of her mouth quirked up in a smile. "Besides, I'm getting a home remodel out of the deal." After a short pause she continued, her tone serious. "You have no idea what that means to me, what a relief it is to have you here."

He lifted a brow. He wasn't the only good contractor in the Fort Myers/Cape Coral area. He was giving her a deal, but something told him there was more behind her relief than getting quality work at a reasonable price. Whatever it was, he'd probably never know. She'd stashed her secrets behind such thick walls it would take a chisel and crowbar to get to them. Or a jackhammer.

Much later Cody lay in bed, still awake. He'd flopped from one side to the other for the past hour and a half, unable to get comfortable. It wasn't the bed's fault. The mattress was the right firmness. The temperature was perfect, too. He just couldn't shut down his thoughts. If he was home, he'd have a bowl of cereal, maybe watch some late-night TV.

If he was home, he wouldn't still be awake.

Here, there were too many things to occupy his mind. Opa and Mimi were totally different from his own grandparents. But they reminded him so much of them, he couldn't talk with them without the void Pops had left almost consuming him.

Knowing their beautiful granddaughter was sleeping at the end of the hall didn't help. Several times over the past few years, he'd have given anything for an opportunity to spend so much time with her. Now it was bittersweet torment as he fought the emotions her nearness resurrected. Emotions he had no business feeling.

The mental battles kept sleep from coming. He'd gotten close once. His thoughts had grown random, and he'd slid down the slippery slope of unconsciousness. Then the squeal of tires and the image of his truck slamming into the concrete barrier had jarred him awake. The trip back over the bridge this afternoon had shaken him more than he wanted to admit.

He flopped onto his other side and rearranged the sheet. When he grew still again, a soft, high-pitched whine broke the silence. He held his breath and listened. A few seconds later it happened again.

He tensed, every sense on full alert. The doors and windows were locked, the alarm set. But was Alcee trying to alert them to danger?

He threw back the sheet and sprang from the bed. When he opened the door, the dog was whining in earnest. She was in the master bedroom. There were other sounds, too, thrashing, as if someone was struggling.

Then a moan and a whimper sent his heart into his throat. Something was wrong with Erin.

He charged down the hall at a full run. Her door was open. Two night-lights illuminated the room with a soft glow. The same glow came from the bathroom.

He cast frantic glances around. Except for her dog, Erin was alone. Alcee lay on the bed, paws on Erin's chest. The dog's head swiveled toward him, and her dark eyes begged him to do something.

Erin tossed her head side to side, another long moan escaping her mouth. It was only a nightmare.

"Erin." He rushed to her side, grasped her shoulders and shook her. "Erin, wake up. It's just a dream."

A strangled scream escaped, and her fist connected with his jaw. He stumbled away from her until his back met the chest of drawers.

Erin bolted upright. She held the sheet clutched to her chest, which rose and fell with every jagged breath. Her green eyes were wide, her hair a tangled mass around her face and shoulders. She was unguarded, vulnerable. And absolutely beautiful.

He dragged his gaze from her face and fixed it on the nightstand next to her. A lamp sat in the center, next to it a water bottle and a book titled *Jesus Calling*.

"You were having a nightmare. I think Alcee was trying to wake you up."

The dog plopped herself across Erin's lap. Erin wrapped both arms around her and rocked back and forth, holding on as if she were drowning and Alcee was her lifeline. It was like dusk in the room, or the beginning moments of sunrise. Who slept with three night-lights?

Someone who was afraid of the dark.

His heart twisted at the fear lingering in her eyes, and he moved closer. When he reached her bedside, he stood still, arms tense with the effort of keeping them at his sides when he longed to draw her into a protective embrace.

But it wouldn't be welcome. He knew without asking. Her dog was providing the comfort he wanted to give.

Her rocking slowed and stopped. How often did Alcee have to chase away the terrors that lurked in her mind?

"What happened? What were you dreaming?"

"I just had a nightmare." Her gaze dipped to her dog, still in her lap. She made a long stroke down Alcee's back, then reversed the motion, burying her fingers in the thick white fur.

"That must have been one doozy of a dream."

She shrugged. "Just an ordinary nightmare. It's not a big deal."

He pressed a hand to the side of his face. "My jaw would beg to differ."

"I'm sorry I hit you. For future reference, never grab someone who's having a nightmare."

Yeah, he knew that about people suffering from PTSD. Like soldiers who'd seen the horrors of battle. Not ordinary people.

But nothing about Erin had ever been ordinary.

She wasn't military. She hadn't seen war. But apparently, sometime during the past twelve years, she'd experienced her own terrors.

SIX

Cody sat at Erin's dining room table, his computer in front of him. A TV played in the background, the sound coming from the slightly open door of the mother-in-law suite. Except for dinnertime, which they all shared together, Mimi and Opa stayed in their quarters. Alcee had the run of the place and hung out with whoever would give her the most attention.

As he'd promised Erin, Cody had spent the day yesterday coming up with kitchen ideas. Last night they'd gone to Lowe's together and picked out appliances and selected several flooring samples. They'd also planned meals for the next week, and since Erin had the day off today, she was at Publix tackling the lengthy grocery list while Cody worked on cabinet design.

He made several clicks with the mouse, typing in intermittent commands, and a drawing took shape on the screen. Erin had chosen a style she liked from the photos in his portfolio, and he'd taken measurements and done rough sketches. But the two- and three-D renderings he was doing in AutoCAD would let her visualize the image he already had in his mind. It would also give his cabinet guy something easier to work with than the scribbles on the legal pad sitting next to his computer.

Once he finished the kitchen remodel, Erin wanted to modernize the bathrooms, then the rest of the house. The mother-in-law suite would be last, long after Mimi and Opa returned to their home in LaBelle.

The way things were going with the investigation, he'd be living at Erin's indefinitely. Everything was at a standstill. Police hadn't found the Camry, and the traps they'd laid yesterday getting his truck to Erin's had come to naught. No one had showed the slightest bit of interest.

Tracing the phone number of the alleged Detective Roland had led nowhere. The call had come from a burner phone. They'd interviewed the developer also, and none of his associates matched the description of the guy in the hospital.

Alcee slipped through the open door, announcing her presence with the tap of her claws against the linoleum floor.

Cody looked away from his work. "Hey, girl. Are you coming for another visit?"

She tilted her head and lifted an ear.

"Mimi and Opa aren't giving you enough love?"

She tipped her head in the other direction, and that ear lifted. Erin had said she was smart. Cody had no idea how much she understood, but she made it look convincing.

He scratched her neck and jaw, and she pressed her head into his hand. When he stopped, instead of lying next to him, she put a paw in his lap.

He checked the time on his computer. Eleven. She wasn't due to eat for another hour.

YOU pick your books – WE pay for everything.

You get up to FOUR New Books and TWO Mystery Gifts...absolutely FREE

Dear Reader,

I am writing to announce the launch of a huge **FREE BOOKS GIVEAWAY**... and to let you know that YOU are entitled to choose up to FOUR fantastic books that WE pay for.

Try **Love Inspired® Romance Larger-Print** books and fall in love with inspirational romances that take you on an uplifting journey of faith, forgiveness and hope.

Try **Love Inspired® Suspense Larger-Print** books where courage and optimism unite in stories of faith and love in the face of danger.

Or TRY BOTH!

In return, we ask just one favor: Would you please participate in our brief Reader Survey? We'd love to hear from you.

This FREE BOOKS GIVEAWAY means that we pay for *everything!* We'll even cover the shipping, and no purchase is necessary, now or later. So please return your survey today. You'll get **Two Free Books** and **Two Mystery Gifts** from each series to try, altogether worth over **$20!**

Sincerely

Pam Powers

Pam Powers
For Harlequin Reader Service

Complete the survey below and return it today to receive up to 4 FREE BOOKS and FREE GIFTS guaranteed!

"What do you want, girl? Do you need to go out?"

She barked once and trotted to the sliding glass door. He rose to let her into the fenced backyard. She would paw at the door when she was ready to come inside again.

After completing his drawing, Cody lifted both arms and arched his back over the chair. He'd slept well last night. After the previous night, he'd been too exhausted to do anything but. Erin had slept well, too. At least, she claimed she had. But even if her nightmare had returned, she wasn't likely to tell him about it. The Erin of old had been an open book, guard down, the world her playground. That Erin no longer existed.

He clicked the mouse and sent what he'd done to the printer in the middle bedroom. With his tools in his truck, his blank invoices and estimate forms in his computer bag, and his laptop connected to Erin's printer, he was ready for business.

His phone rang, interrupting his thoughts. Erin's name displayed on the screen.

"I'm getting ready to check out. Anything else you want me to get while I'm here?"

"I don't think so. That list we made last night was pretty extensive."

"Tell me about it. My cart's heaping. Food preparation for four is a little different from food preparation for one."

A lot more expensive, too. But they'd all agreed to do an even four-way split—half the bill paid by Mimi and Opa and a quarter each by him and Erin.

"Sounds like you'll make it home before I leave." He was meeting Bobby for lunch at Zaxby's, then stopping by Sherwin-Williams for paint chips. "You're welcome to join us." He laughed. "If I bring a woman along, maybe Bobby will stop trying to match me up with his coworker."

Her laughter joined his. "Thanks for the invite. Although I'd love to be able to bail you out, I think I'll just have lunch with Mimi and Opa. Since your friend's a cop, I'd say you're in good hands."

As he disconnected the call, Alcee scratched against the sliding glass door frame. He slid the door back on its track. "Come on, girl."

She bounded in, tail wagging. Lunchtime was close, and she knew it. The dog had a built-in clock. Cody walked into the kitchen and picked up the porcelain bowl. The white dish with a big blue paw print in the bottom was licked clean.

"Are you ready to eat?" Her head tilted again, and her ear lifted when he said *eat*. That was a word she *did* understand, like almost every other pet in America.

He took a can of Purina ONE from the pantry and popped the top. After he'd dumped the contents into the dish, he glanced at the clock hanging on the opposite wall. He was feeding her fifteen minutes early. If it was a problem, he'd stick to a stricter schedule in the future.

A short time later Erin arrived home with the back of her RAV4 filled with groceries. He met her outside and, after looping several bags over each arm, nodded down at what he held. "You can start putting everything away, since you know where it goes. I'll tote the rest in."

When they finished, it was time for him to leave. He picked up his keys and stuffed his phone into his pocket. "I'll see you in a couple of hours."

"If you see anything suspicious, or are even slightly uneasy, call the police. Then get a hold of me."

He grinned. "You *are* the police. So is Bobby."

"Someone on duty whose sirens and lights can get them there in a hurry."

When he arrived at Zaxby's, Bobby was already inside waiting near the door. The larger man clapped Cody on the shoulder in greeting, and he winced. He was still sore, as much from slamming into the concrete barrier as spending the night trapped in the collapsed building. The dive in the parking lot hadn't helped, either. Neither had being blown halfway across his front yard.

But Bobby knew none of that. Cody had gotten a hold of him yesterday to let him know he'd relocated to Fort Myers and wouldn't need the ride from his house. He would fill him in on everything else over lunch. Soon, they were seated at a table, two plates of wings and fries in front of them.

Cody picked up a fry and dipped it in ketchup. "Did you hear about the apartment building collapsing in Bokeelia, on Pine Island?"

"Not only did I hear about it, I was on duty, keeping people who didn't belong from venturing back there. I didn't see the story air, but I heard the collapse was intentional."

"It was. I was inside when it went down, even spent a little time in the hospital with a concussion and some broken ribs."

"Whoa. I had no idea that was you. What were you doing there?"

"Trying to convince my stubborn grandfather to evacuate."

Bobby shook his head. "You don't look much worse for wear. How about your pops?"

Cody pressed his lips together. "He didn't make it."

"Ah, man, that's rough. Sorry to hear that."

Cody nodded his thanks. "What have you heard about the case?"

"Nothing. Being in patrol, I'm not involved in homicide investigations."

As they ate, Cody filled him in on everything that had happened. Finally, Bobby sat back and shook his head. "You've gotten yourself tangled up in a mess."

"I know." He was still having a hard time wrapping his mind around it. "I'm not used to having people out to get me. I get along with everybody." At least, once he'd gotten through his troubled adolescent and early teen years. "The last time I had an enemy was in ninth grade when someone tripped me in the cafeteria and I spilled Kool-Aid on Jimmy Thompson's new Izod shirt."

Bobby laughed, then grew silent, thinking as he finished off the last of his chicken. "Have you checked with the planning department to see if the developer sought approval for anything there?"

Cody picked up one of his wings and took a bite. His plate was still half-full. He'd been the one doing almost all the talking.

"I don't know if anyone has thought of that. As a contractor, I know the people there pretty well. I'll see what I can find out. If he's already been to the planning people, he's pretty serious about buying." Of course, the offer Erin said the developer had made to Whitmer showed some pretty strong determination.

"So where are you staying? You said somewhere here in Fort Myers."

"Yeah. I'm staying with someone I just reconnected with, who also happens to be one of the detectives working the case."

"That's convenient. He's letting you live there until this gets wrapped up?"

"Not *he*—*she*. And yes, she's letting me stay until this is over. Actually, she's not giving me a choice. Everything that's happened has her pretty worried."

Bobby grinned. "Hmm. Sounds promising."

Cody shook his head. "It's not like that. There's no romance going on. I've got my own room and so do her grandparents."

Bobby had been around for the implosion of Cody's marriage and had been on a mission ever since to secure him a happily-ever-after. Cody had made it clear he wasn't interested, but his friend still hadn't given up. The man wasn't dense, just determined.

Bobby shrugged. "No romance now, and grandparents to chaperone. But you never know where things might lead." He waggled his brows, which looked more silly than anything. Knowing Bobby, the effect was intentional.

Yeah, one never knew where things might lead. But some paths were so unlikely it didn't make sense to even consider them. Neither he nor Erin had any intention of letting down their guard. He didn't know what was behind her resistance, but he understood his own. He'd had enough people he loved walk away that he wasn't interested in going another round. Life alone was pretty good, as long as he stayed busy and never dwelled on what he'd lost.

Bobby crumpled up his napkin and dropped it on the empty plate. "Well, if things don't work out with this lady, I can always introduce you to my cute coworker."

"Sorry, I'm going to pass on both."

Bobby's brow creased. "Actually, if you were conscious when they pulled you out of the rubble, you might have already met her. Cute lady about this tall." He held up a hand. "White German shepherd dog."

"Erin? That's who I'm staying with."

Bobby bellowed with laughter, slapping the table and struggling to catch his breath.

Cody frowned. "You wanna tell me what's so funny so we can both enjoy the joke?"

Bobby gradually got control of himself. "Erin Jeffries is the woman I've been trying to introduce you to."

"You told me she was in patrol with you."

"She was. Then she moved to detective. I guess I didn't tell you that part." He chuckled a couple more times.

"Do you work with somebody named Joe?"

"You got a last name?"

Cody shook his head. "He's been trying to match Erin up with a friend of his. She keeps turning him down, but the guy's persistent."

The laughter bubbled up again.

Cody waited, his frown deepening. "I'm glad you're finding this so entertaining."

"Sorry, I can't help it." He made a valiant attempt at seriousness, but his lips quivered with the effort. "I'm Joe."

"Huh?" He and Bobby had been friends for four years. How would Cody not know that?

"My given name is Joseph Robert Morris Junior. With my dad being Joe, it was too confusing having two of us in the house, so I was Bobby. Everywhere I've worked, though, they've called me Joseph or Joe." A couple more chuckles escaped. "As much as I wanted to introduce you guys and got nowhere, your paths still managed to cross. God does work in mysterious ways."

Cody's frown returned. God probably didn't have anything to do with it. But crediting the coincidences of life with the intervention of God was what he'd expect from Bobby. His friend had invited him to several of his church's activities over the years. Cody had turned down those invitations the same way he'd rejected the matchmaking attempts—with a good-natured but firm *no*.

He didn't need church. He was doing all right. He had his work, his hobbies, his friends and his home. But he wasn't just wrapped up in his own life. He'd always been generous with his money, making regular donations to several charitable organizations, at least until his ex-wife wiped him out. That generosity had to rack up some brownie points with the man upstairs. If some people needed more to feel fulfilled, he understood. But the whole religion scene wasn't for him.

Cody had almost finished his meal when a buzz notified him of an incoming text. He held up an index finger. "I need to take this, in case it's Erin."

At least now Bobby would leave him alone about the pretty fellow law-enforcement officer. Or maybe not. Now that they were living under the same roof, he'd probably be even more relentless.

Cody pulled out his phone. The notification wasn't from Erin. "Finally. I've had protein powder on back order since two days before the storm. It just got delivered an hour ago." He pocketed the phone. "Would you mind running me by there to grab it? Then you can drop me back by here."

Erin wouldn't like it, but he couldn't expect Lee County or Cape Coral PD to act as errand boys.

Bobby's eyebrows dipped toward his nose. "You sure it's not a trap? It's definitely your package?"

"Yeah. The notification came from the company."

Bobby nodded, but deep vertical lines still marked the space between his eyebrows. "I think you should check with Erin."

Cody scowled. He hadn't asked for permission to go somewhere since he was a kid. But Bobby was right. Erin was doing everything in her power to keep him safe. She deserved to know if he was getting ready to do something reckless. Besides, he'd already vowed he'd listen to her from now on.

He pulled his phone back out and dialed Erin. Her "hello" sounded anxious. Of course it would. She'd told him to call her at the first sign of danger.

"Everything's all right. I just wanted to let you know about another stop I need to make."

"O-kay." The anxiousness had turned to hesitation.

"My protein powder finally arrived. I was going to have Bobby run me by to pick it up."

"Are you trying to get yourself killed?"

He ignored the sharpness in her tone. "We'll be in his truck. I'll even stay inside. Bobby can jump out and grab the box." He paused. "No one knows I'm going over there."

"No one except whoever might have seen that package being delivered."

"Do you really think someone's watching my house twenty-four/seven?"

"Can you guarantee someone isn't?"

No, he couldn't guarantee anything, except that less than two weeks had passed since the destruction of his grandfather's apartment building, and he already couldn't wait to get his life back.

"Don't forget, Bobby's a police officer." His arguments were losing their conviction.

"And he's bringing along an explosives detection dog?"

The last of his resistance fled like air escaping from a balloon.

"I didn't think so." She paused, but not for long. "Some guy blew the supports out from under your grandfather's apartment building, then blew up your rental car. You know how easy it would be to cut open your package, put something inside, rig it to explode the moment the box is opened, then seal it back up?"

He nodded, his lower lip pulled between his teeth. Okay, he was properly chastised.

"Go on to my place. I'll call it in and have a dog check it out before anyone touches it. If it's clean, we'll have it delivered here."

Cody agreed and disconnected the call. Two wings still sat on his plate, but he'd lost his appetite. He said his farewells to Bobby, promising to keep him posted, then walked to his truck. As he slid into the seat, a bolt of panic shot through him. His neighbor Jack was keeping an eye on his place. If he noticed the package on his porch, he'd pick it up and take it home for safekeeping.

He brought up Jack's number and pressed the call icon. After Jack's voice-mail message played, Cody left his own message and then sent a text as backup. All he could do was hope Jack saw the text or missed call before noticing the package. Or that the police arrived there first.

Cody stopped at Sherwin-Williams and gathered

paint chips in the color combinations he and Erin had discussed. Then he headed for her house. Three blocks away the light in front of him turned red, and his phone buzzed with an incoming text.

It was from Erin. Just two words. But they sent a waterfall of dread crashing over him.

Dog alerted.

Cody held open the glass door leading into the building department, and Erin walked through with a nod of thanks. It was her investigation, but Cody was a gentleman.

Friday's package situation had turned out all right. The authorities had evacuated the surrounding houses and defused the bomb without incident.

Since then, she'd thanked God several times that Cody had called her instead of heading over there. Cody probably hadn't. She'd invited him to go to church with her and Mimi and Opa, and he'd declined, saying he needed to get some estimates finished. That was all right. Cody was in the same place she'd been four months earlier. Courtney hadn't given up on her, and she wouldn't give up on Cody.

The killer had acted fast. In the less than two-hour time frame between when the package was delivered and the police arrived with the bomb detection dog, he'd sliced the tape on top, inserted the bomb and taped it back up.

If Cody had opened it, he'd have been killed instantly. If he'd waited until he got to her house, he might have taken Mimi and Opa out, too. Or if he'd opened it in Joe's truck, they'd both have been blown to bits.

At the thought of the Lee County officer, a smile threatened. All along, Cody was the friend Joe had hounded her about meeting. What would've happened if she'd given in and agreed to meet him, if they'd both given in? Where would they be today, enjoying a solid friendship, having moved past their history and settled into an easy camaraderie? Or would their relationship have grown into something more serious? The latter seemed like nothing but a fantasy, far out of reach, but a part of her wanted to believe it was possible.

Some relationships made a lasting impact, causing change that endured for a lifetime. She'd experienced the negative side of that. But what about change for the good? Could a man like Cody undo all the damage of the past, or was she beyond that point? Would he even want to try? He'd suffered his own wounds.

She squared her shoulders and shook off the thoughts. Right now they were at the Lee County Building Department, seeking out details on the plans Donovan Development had for the land the apartment building had occupied. As they walked toward the planning department, Cody greeted each of the employees they passed. Then they sat to wait their turn. Erin didn't expect any surprises. Donovan had already given them the abridged version of what he'd hoped to do, plans he'd scrapped when Whitmer hadn't been willing to sell.

A short time later one of the clerks called Cody by name. After the woman made introductions, they both sat.

Cody leaned forward to rest an arm on her desk. "I talked to Sheila yesterday. She was going to pull the preliminary plans for the project Donovan Development had planned on Pine Island."

The woman rose—Tamara, according to Cody's introduction and her nameplate. When she returned, she handed him a roll of blueprint-size pages. He spread them out on the desk and began reviewing them.

Erin turned her attention to Tamara. "How well do you know Donovan?"

"Just on a professional level. He's been in here a few times for different projects and things he's doing."

"What's he like to work with?"

"He's all right. A little pushy sometimes, but he's a powerful man. Probably used to getting his own way."

Cody rolled up a page, and Erin looked at what was beneath. It was an artist's rendering of what appeared to be a resort. A hotel rose from the center, eight or ten stories tall, with a pool, a couple of restaurants, miniature golf and walkways that curved through tropical plants and a water feature.

Erin lifted her brows. "All that on one acre?"

"No." Cody rolled that sheet around the first. "This incorporates the properties on either side, too."

Erin nodded. "Then he'd own everything from Charlotte Harbor on the north end of Boca Vista to Back Bay on the south."

"With nothing across the street except marshland bordering Charlotte Harbor to the west."

Erin leaned back in her chair. "That's if all three property owners agreed to sell." The owners on either side of Whitmer's apartments hadn't mentioned being approached. Of course, no one had asked. Law enforcement's focus had been on what those owners may have seen the day of the storm.

Cody finished reviewing the plans and handed them

back to Tamara. After they thanked her for her time, they made their way back to the front of the building.

Erin stepped into the parking lot and clicked her fob. "Donovan put a lot of time and money into his plan. I agree with your friend in there. Men that powerful are used to getting their own way."

Cody slid into the passenger seat. "If the two owners on the end agreed to sell, Whitmer would have been the only thing holding up a lucrative deal. And if those offers were as good as the one made to Whitmer, they wouldn't have been happy about him throwing a monkey wrench in the thing. Looks like motive to me."

"But would they have the means or incentive to go to this extent?"

"Money is a good motivator, especially if someone is desperate enough."

"True." Erin cranked the car and backed out of the parking space. "How well do you know the neighbors on either side of your grandfather's apartment building?"

"I know the couple on the left pretty well. They're older. Not as old as Pops. Maybe in their sixties. But they befriended him, even had him over for meals several times."

"What about the owners on the other side?"

"According to Pops, the other neighbor's a single guy. I saw him in passing a couple of times. I waved, and he waved back."

"I think I saw him the day you were getting your pops's things. Dark, short-cropped hair, clean-shaven, drives a red Tacoma?"

"Yeah. Looks nothing like our suspect."

But that didn't mean he didn't hire someone to set the charges. She pulled into traffic, then glanced over at Cody. "I'm going to drop you off at home and go talk to them." By the end of the afternoon, she hoped to find out just how desperate those neighbors might be.

A short time later she backed out of her drive, a grilled cheese sandwich and a plastic container with apple slices lying on the seat next to her, a travel mug of tea in the cup holder, all prepared by Cody. By the time she reached Pine Island, both the food and the tea were gone. She made her turn onto Boca Vista Court and drove to the end.

The red Tacoma she'd watched roll past a couple of weeks earlier was sitting in the drive. She rang the bell and the door swung inward.

"Jordan McIntyre?"

"Yes."

She introduced herself to the man she recognized as the Tacoma's driver. "Can I ask you a few questions?"

"Sure." He motioned her inside.

As he led her to the living room, she took in her surroundings. A leather sectional occupied two walls, and heavy oak bookcases framed a large picture window. Interspersed among the books were vases, figurines and other collectibles.

Pictures graced another wall, an eleven-by-fourteen wedding photo in the center. Judging from the hairstyles and the yellow tint, the picture was at least forty years old. Many of the others were studio portraits, their subject a boy, infant to high school age. Nothing about the space said *midthirties single guy*.

He swept his arm toward the sectional. "Have a seat."

She complied, and he sat at the other end.

"How long have you lived here?"

"This time? Four years."

"Before that?"

"Wisconsin. But this is where I grew up."

She nodded. "Your parents transferred the house to you five years ago, right?" She knew the answer. She'd already looked up the information on the property appraiser's website.

"Yeah."

"Is there a mortgage?"

"No. Mom and Dad paid it off before they retired."

"Where are they now?"

"Montana, I think. They bought a motor home and have been traveling the continent for the past four years." He grinned, showing straight white teeth. "Spending my inheritance."

"What do you do for a living?"

"Framing carpentry. I work for Coventry Construction."

Hmm. One of the contractors who did work for Donovan Development. "How long have you worked for them?"

"I just started ten days ago."

Okay, maybe not.

"They offered me two dollars an hour more than I was getting with Gersham Contracting."

"Why aren't you working for them today?"

"I was this morning. Finished a job, and the next one won't be ready to start till tomorrow. There was a glitch on getting materials delivered. The hurricane has everyone backlogged."

"What year is that Tacoma out there?"

"2017." He smiled again, his demeanor personable. "Three more payments and it'll be all mine."

She returned his smile. "That's always a good feeling. Did anyone from Donovan Development ever contact you about buying this place?"

"Yeah, Donovan himself. He offered fifty percent over market value. Even though it's mine, I didn't think I should unload it without talking to Mom and Dad. But they were good with it, so I told Donovan I'd take his offer."

"What happened with the deal?"

"It fell through, or at least got stalled. The people on the other end agreed to sell, too, but the guy in the middle didn't. It was all or nothing, so the sale never happened. Or hasn't yet."

"How did that make you feel?"

"I was okay either way. I like it here. It's comfortable and quiet. My boat is right out there, tied to the dock on Back Bay. And the place is paid for. What more could I ask?"

By the time Erin left, she'd eliminated Jordan McIntyre as someone likely to be behind the setting of the charges. He had a good job, a house free and clear and a decent truck almost paid for. Nothing about the man seemed desperate.

The other stop didn't provide any likely suspects, either. As soon as Dave and Margaret Smith opened the door, Erin recognized them from her church, though she didn't know them well. That in itself didn't kick them off the possible suspect list. After all, serial killer Dennis Rader not only attended church but was also president of his church council.

But the conversation Erin had with them assured her they shouldn't be on her list of suspects. Dave had retired two years ago from his job as an engineer in upper New York State. He and his wife were enjoying their dream of living near the water in a warm climate. When Donovan had added another $50,000 to his already generous offer, they'd agreed to sell, but they'd been relieved when the deal had fallen through.

Erin made her way off Pine Island and headed toward Fort Myers. She wouldn't eliminate either of the neighbors as suspects completely until they'd been thoroughly checked out, but in the meantime, it seemed she'd just hit two more dead ends. Which meant investigators had been working on the case for almost two weeks and had no solid suspect.

A killer was still on the loose, one who had Cody in his sights.

SEVEN

Cody's eyes snapped open. Something had disturbed him. He lay on his left side in the darkened room, the chest of drawers in the corner barely visible. A soft glow came from behind him.

He rolled onto his other side. His phone lay on the nightstand, its screen illuminated. It was probably a text notification that had awoken him. He swiped the screen. Yes, one unread text.

Two taps later, he bolted from the bed, eyes still fixed on the message:

R U back home? Smoke coming from bedroom window.

He keyed in a frantic reply:

No, calling 911. Be there in 20 min.

The return message came back moments later:

Already called. Just get over here.

He flipped the switch, then squinted in the stark

white light. He couldn't show up on the other side of the county in his gym shorts and barefoot. The jeans and T-shirt he'd worn yesterday were draped over the back of the upholstered chair. He struggled into them with shaking hands, then put on his tennis shoes.

When he'd finished, his pulse was still racing, his thoughts flying in a thousand different directions. He'd asked Jack to keep an eye on his place, but he hadn't expected the man to send him a middle-of-the-night text like this. His home, his workshop, all his possessions, the things he'd retrieved from Pops's place—would anything even be salvageable?

He snatched his keys and wallet and ran for the front door. Alcee met him there. As he punched in the code to disarm the alarm, she looked up at him and released a whine. He rearmed the system, and the series of beeps that followed ratcheted up his tension. The vise that had clamped down on his chest the moment he read Jack's text refused to release.

When he swung the door inward, Alcee forced her way into the opening and erupted in a frenzy of frantic barking.

"Alcee, hush." She was wasting valuable time.

He took a deep breath and tried to calm himself down. Firefighters were on their way, maybe even already there, sending powerful streams of water shooting into his home, dousing the flames. There was nothing he could do till they finished.

The place was likely crawling with cops. He'd be safe there. Unless…

A block of dread slid down his throat and congealed in his stomach. He closed the door and pulled the phone from his pocket. Had he paid attention to the sender when reading the text? Or had he, fresh out of a sound sleep, just read the message and panicked?

The conversation was displayed on the screen. Jack's name wasn't. The number had Cape Coral's 239 area code but wasn't programmed in his contacts.

Cody sank onto the couch, the phone still clutched in his hand. Alcee approached and rested her head on his leg, as if trying to console him. It didn't help. The killer had his address and phone number and had played him. And Cody had almost fallen for it. Stupid, stupid, stupid.

The living room light came on, and he heaved a sigh. Now he'd have Erin's chastisement to add to his own. He deserved both.

Erin stepped into the room, eyebrows drawn together and hair in disarray above her silk pajamas. "I heard the alarm beeping, like it had been reset, and Alcee barking. Were you trying to leave?"

"I got a text that my house was on fire."

"From who?"

"I thought it was from my neighbor."

"So you were going to leave to check it out all by yourself. I'm really starting to think you have a death wish." Her voice held an uncharacteristic shrillness. She was going to wake up Mimi and Opa if she didn't tone it down.

"Alcee stopped me."

Erin planted her hands on her hips. "At least someone in this house has some sense."

Ouch. That hurt. He brought up the keypad on his phone. "I'm calling 911. There's a good chance the killer's waiting for me. The police might be able to catch him."

He'd just finished explaining everything to the dispatcher when the door leading to the mother-in-law suite creaked open the rest of the way, and Opa stepped into the living room.

"Everything okay?"

Erin's head swiveled in his direction. "Cody got a text that his house is on fire."

Opa's eyes widened. "Oh, no."

"We think it's a setup." Though her grandparents didn't know the details, Erin had told them that Cody had witnessed a crime and had to hide out for a while.

For several moments Opa stood looking at them. Then he nodded and disappeared back into the suite with his wife.

"How did Alcee know I was in danger?"

Erin sank onto the couch next to him and reached over to stroke Alcee's head. "We have no idea the things animals sense. But you were probably putting out some frantic vibes. She'd have known something was wrong, even without being aware of the specific dangers."

Cody nodded, his hand joining Erin's on Alcee's head. Yeah, he'd definitely put out some bad vibes. He'd been so panicked, his brain had disengaged. If the dog hadn't slowed him down enough to stop and think, he'd have charged right into danger. Alcee had just saved his life for the second time.

No, probably the third.

The toxicology report on the soup hadn't come back yet, so he had no proof. But despite what he'd said to Erin about being a show-me kind of guy, he couldn't deny it any longer. The maintenance guy had put something in his soup. Something intended to kill him. It had been the first attempt on his life, and Alcee had saved him.

Tonight the creep had crafted another way to try to get to him. And Alcee had come through again.

Darkness settled over everything, smothering every last sliver of light. Erin's heart beat against her rib cage, and her breaths came in short, shallow gasps.

It was a dream, wasn't it? Yes. *Just a dream.* It was one she'd had so many times she'd trained herself to recognize it.

But did it always feel this real? Maybe this time it wasn't a dream. Maybe it was actually happening.

No. She asked herself that question every time, because it always felt real. Someone said people didn't feel pain when dreaming. They were wrong.

Because she felt everything in agonizing detail. The gag in her mouth. The ropes biting into her ankles and wrists. Even the bruises from where vengeful fists had taken out their anger on almost every square inch of her body.

He was nearby. She could hear his breathing. Clothing rustled. Was he shifting positions or preparing to approach?

She lay as still as if she were dead. Maybe if she didn't move, he'd forget about her. How long had it been? How much longer would it be? Nights slipped into days, which slid into more nights, the blindfold making every hour the same as the one before it. The only difference was the level of pain.

How long would it take for her spirit to slip peacefully out of her body?

The rustle grew louder. Then there were footsteps. Rough hands grabbed her, pulling her to her feet. No, he'd never let her slip peacefully away. When her legs buckled, he dragged her some distance and gave her a hard shove. A couch caught her backward tumble.

She trembled, waiting for the first blow. It came, and a scream clawed its way up her throat. How many fruitless screams had she released into the duct tape binding her mouth?

Another blow, another muffled scream. And tears she couldn't stop.

Then there was a whimper, different from her own. Light pressure against her chest. A wet tongue traced a path up her cheek. Those sensations weren't terrifying. In spite of the darkness, they were soothing.

And a male voice. Not *his*. This one belonged to someone kind and gentle. He was calling her name, assuring her she was safe, telling her to wake up.

She opened her eyes and bolted upright with a gasp. Two paws slid down her abdomen and into her lap. The darkness was gone in an instant. The remnants of the dream would take much longer to dissipate.

Alcee moved closer and pressed the side of her head to Erin's chest. Movement in her peripheral vision drew a gasp.

Cody stood two feet from the side of her bed, one hand raised. "It's all right. I was trying to wake you up. Alcee and I both were." One side of his mouth lifted. "She's the brave one. I kept my distance."

She gave him a shaky half smile. "That's probably smart."

All the times Alcee had brought her out of a nightmare, Erin had never hit her. In her unconscious but frantic state, she'd somehow known her dog posed no threat.

"Sorry I woke you up." She scooted backward to

rest against the headboard, pulse still racing. Alcee followed. Erin wrapped her arms around Alcee's middle and buried her face in the fur at the dog's neck. Erin still needed her, and the dog knew it.

Alcee wasn't an emotional support animal in an official sense. She'd come through the National Training Center in Santa Paula, known for recognizing the potential in shelter dogs and training them in search and rescue. It hadn't taken long to learn that Alcee helped her with her PTSD, waking her from nightmares, then calming her afterward.

When Erin had made her move to Florida, Sunnyvale had allowed her to take Alcee with her and join the volunteer group, Peace River K-9 Search and Rescue. If Erin had been forced to leave her dog, she still would've chosen to be near her grandparents, but the decision would've shredded her heart.

Cody moved closer. "Is it okay if I sit?"

She nodded. It was okay as long as he didn't pry. She hadn't told anyone about those terrifying ten days. Well, she'd told the counselors. But that didn't count.

It also didn't help.

No, that assessment wasn't fair. The counseling had reduced the frequency of the nightmares, just not made them go away. She'd expected the latter.

Cody seated himself near the foot of the bed, facing her. She was probably a mess—eyes wild and hair sticking out at odd angles like a knotted, tangled bird's nest. No fewer than three night-lights illuminated the room and announced her weakness. She was a cop, someone whose job put her in the path of danger, and she was scared of the dark.

She should feel embarrassed. At least awkward. But

with her dog lying in her lap, and Cody sitting three feet away staring at her with those warm dark eyes, she just felt…safe.

"By the way, two nightmares in less than a week is not the norm for me."

"One nightmare a month is too many."

She'd be happy with one a month. Twelve per year. She could handle that. "I think my subconscious is latching on to all the stuff that's happening to you. You're the one with someone trying to kill you, and I'm the one having nightmares about it." She laughed, but it didn't sound natural, even to herself.

Two soft raps sounded against the open door, and she started. It was only Opa.

"Everything okay? I thought I heard you scream."

She smiled wryly. She'd insisted they leave their door open so they could call if they needed her. They'd been concerned about disturbing her. It hadn't happened yet. But she'd woken them twice.

"I just had a bad dream."

Her grandparents knew about her nightmares, even the story behind them. Opa nodded, his gaze shifting to Cody, then back to her again. "It looks like you're in good hands, so I'm going back to bed."

When he left, Cody studied her. His eyes bored into her, as if he was looking past her walls to the brokenness she kept hidden. "What happened?"

She tensed. "What do you mean?"

"What did you experience that was so terrifying your mind keeps taking you back to the same dark place?"

His gaze held sympathy, even pleading. It weakened her resolve. But only for a moment. If weeks of counseling couldn't banish the nightmares, neither would talking to Cody. She had her medicine. It was Alcee.

And prayer. It calmed her thoughts and helped her fall asleep. But the nightmares hadn't stopped, and they weren't any less terrifying. She'd asked God more than once to take them away. So far He hadn't. Maybe they were like Paul's thorn in the flesh, something to keep her dependent on Him.

Through it all, she was learning trust, the confidence that God would protect her, not only physically, but mentally and emotionally, too. She still had a long way to go. But she was making baby steps. Maybe someday, the night-lights would go off.

She ran her palm down Alcee's back, and the dog released a contented sigh.

"Erin?"

She lifted her gaze to his.

"When the case is solved and I return home, I'd like for us to stay friends."

She nodded. She didn't want to let him go, either.

"I want to know you." He rested a hand on her lower leg where it lay hidden by the sheet. "You're not the same carefree girl I met twelve years ago. Something changed you. Help me understand."

She closed her eyes. His hand felt warm through the sheet. The heat spread, chasing away some of the chill that still lingered.

But he was asking for something she couldn't give, to lower her walls and let him in. But her walls weren't made of brick and mortar. They were rebar in solid-poured concrete. It really was possible for someone to be too damaged to fix.

"Please, Erin."

When she opened her eyes, she kept her gaze fixed on her dog. Cody wanted friendship. Friends shared secrets, right? Except she hadn't shared this secret with anyone.

Her ex was ten years into a twenty-five-year sentence. But she'd lived the past ten years in a prison of her own. One of fear and regret over the choices she'd made. Maybe in sharing, thirty-year-old Erin would find healing that twenty-year-old Erin hadn't been mature enough to receive.

She kept her eyes cast downward, her fingers entwined in Alcee's fur. "I've made some poor choices."

The first was walking away from Cody. If she hadn't made that decision, her life might have taken a different path, and the other events wouldn't have happened.

"My wife cleared out our bank accounts and took off with her boyfriend. Last I heard, they're backpacking across Europe. I've had my nose to the grindstone ever since. I'm still trying to recover." He released a dry laugh. "Trust me, you don't have a monopoly on bad choices."

"Ever make a choice that almost got you killed?" Okay, bad question. "Not including anything in the past two weeks?"

He didn't answer, just waited for her to continue.

She lifted her gaze to a painting that hung on the opposite wall. "I'd just finished my second year of college. A guy I'd been dating for two months got really possessive. After talking to some friends, I decided to dump him."

Her tone was flat. If she kept the emotion out of her voice, maybe she could keep it out of her heart. Then she'd have a chance of making it through the whole story.

"We'd already made plans to visit his family in Washington to do some hiking, camping and white-water rafting. We were then going to venture up into British Columbia. I didn't want to ruin everyone's vacation, so I went, figuring I'd break up with him when we got back to California."

As she talked, she kept her eyes fixed on the painting. It had been there when she'd bought the house. It was a seascape, but not a Florida one. Waves crashed against cliffs, surf spraying high in the air, wild and harsh and unpredictable. Like life.

"He'd gotten wind of my plans and wasn't willing to let me go. Instead of taking me to his parents' house, we ended up at a remote cabin in the woods. When we got there, it was like something snapped."

A shudder passed through her. Cody moved to sit next to her, lifting Alcee's back end from the bed onto his lap. When he slid his arm between the headboard and her shoulders, she didn't resist. There was something comforting about sitting next to him, being nestled against his side. His strength flowed into her, giving her what she needed to continue.

"As soon as we got there, he started hitting me, punching me in the face and head. I was still in the car, hadn't even released my seat belt." He'd beat her until she lost consciousness, then dragged her inside.

"I woke up on the floor of the cabin, feet bound, hands tied behind my back, and mouth taped so I couldn't scream. I doubt anyone would've heard me, anyway. On the way in, we drove for miles without seeing another house." Never had she felt so alone. Or so utterly hopeless. "Every time I woke up, he'd hit me some more, until I passed out again. I knew I was going to die. More than once, that's what I prayed for."

Cody's arm tensed, and he pulled her more tightly against his side. She turned her face toward him, pressing her cheek into his chest. The terrors lessened their grip on her mind.

"He had me blindfolded the entire time, so I never knew if it was day or night. After I was rescued, I learned I'd been held captive for ten days. I'd drifted in and out of consciousness, but I was always in total blackness. I haven't slept in a dark room since." Even when they'd lost power during the hurricane, she'd kept a battery-operated lantern going all night.

"After it was over, I trained in self-defense, changed my major from chemistry to criminal justice and went to the police academy. Then I settled in Sunnyvale, almost seven hours from my hometown of Anaheim. He's incarcerated, but eventually he'll get out. I'm not making it easy for him to find me."

She leaned away from Cody to meet his eyes. "Now you know why I have no social-media presence."

"I'm so sorry you had to go through that." His jaw was tight, but his eyes were filled with sympathy, even pain, as if he was hurting with her.

She didn't deserve it. "It was stupid of me to go with him. I should have seen the signs."

"We're all allowed mistakes. At some point we have to stop beating ourselves up over them."

"It's hard to forgive yourself when the bad things that happen are your own fault."

A good half minute passed before he spoke again.

"You believe that God forgives you for your mistakes, right?"

"Of course."

"How do you think He feels about you not forgiving yourself?"

She pursed her lips, eyebrows drawn together. She'd never considered that. Somewhere in the Bible she'd read the command to forgive others as God had forgiven her. Did *others* include herself? She didn't have an answer.

He continued, his voice low. "Holding on to the past allows it to keep us in bondage. Maybe healing begins when we stop beating ourselves up." The contemplation in his tone said he wasn't only thinking about her. Maybe he had some regrets of his own.

He lifted his other hand to cup the side of her head. She relaxed against him, enveloped in safety. His heart beat against her ear, sure and steady.

Was he right? Was berating herself for her bad choices stopping her from healing?

She drew in a deep breath but wasn't ready to pull out of his embrace. "Thank you for listening and not judging. Other than my immediate family and my counselors, you're the only one I've ever told this to."

"I appreciate your sharing. It means a lot."

His voice was deeper than usual, making his chest rumble beneath her face. A light scent wafted to her, barely detectable—evergreen, citrus and a hint of spice. Maybe aftershave or body wash used during his evening shower.

He'd said he wanted to remain friends. She'd agreed. But what if she wanted more? Cody made her feel safe, which was more than she could say about some of the men in her life. He would never lay a hand on her. But could she trust him to protect her emotionally, too? What did emotionally safe even feel like?

She pulled away, and he relaxed his arms. The air that moved between them felt suddenly cold. She dipped her head. "It's only three thirty. You could get a few more hours of sleep."

"What about you?"

"I'll be awake for a while." After one of her nightmares, sleep was a long time coming, partly because she fought it, afraid to relinquish control to her subconscious. When she left her subconscious in charge, it sometimes took her places she didn't want to go.

She shrugged. "I'll read. Eventually, I'll fall asleep."

He rose and pulled a chair up next to her bed. "I'll sit with you until you do."

She started to object. But the words never made it past her lips. Protesting would be pointless. Cody knew she needed him, and nothing would dissuade him from being here for her.

She took her reader from the nightstand, where it lay next to her devotional book, then turned on her side, her back to him. He rested a hand on her shoulder, the light pressure a constant reminder that he was here.

Cody being such an intimate part of her life was temporary, tonight's comfort even more so. But that wouldn't stop her from relishing it while it lasted.

EIGHT

Erin sat at her dining room table nursing a cup of coffee. Two books lay open in front of her, her Bible and her devotional book. Courtney had recommended both, telling her to start with the Book of John, then work her way through the rest of the New Testament and read one of the daily devotionals in *Jesus Calling*. Each of the passages was written as if spoken by Jesus Himself, and over the past three months, she'd been amazed at how often the message had been just what she'd needed.

She closed the book and opened her Bible. The early morning was quiet, the other occupants in the house still asleep. The two-legged ones, anyway. When she'd risen, Alcee had followed her out of the room.

Erin hadn't bothered to set the alarm. Today started the Labor Day weekend. She'd put in for four days' vacation so she could go camping with Courtney. Those plans had changed. She didn't feel comfortable leaving Cody that long, especially since Alcee would be with her. Courtney had understood and agreed to reschedule once the case was wrapped up.

Erin took a sip of coffee and then set the mug on the table, leaving her hands wrapped around it. Even though her alarm hadn't gone off, she'd awoken at sunup anyway, rested and refreshed. It helped that last night's sleep had been blessedly dreamless.

The prior morning the blaring alarm had jarred her out of a sound sleep. Her reader had still been in the bed, but the chair next to her had been empty. After unloading her past to Cody, she'd picked up her tablet to read and within ten minutes could no longer hold her eyes open. She never got to sleep that soon after a nightmare. If she said his presence had had nothing to do with it, she'd be lying.

Alcee lifted her head from her food dish and padded over to the table. Erin held the dog's face between her hands. "You're a good girl." She inhaled, then wrinkled her nose. "But you smell like Purina."

Alcee responded with a drawn-out *"Aarrrr."*

"Yes, you do. You need a doggy breath mint."

When Erin looked up, Cody was standing at the edge of the open doorway, grinning.

She returned his smile. "I didn't know you were up."

"I've only been up a few minutes. I didn't announce myself, because I was enjoying your conversation with your dog."

He walked into the kitchen and poured himself a cup of coffee. "Am I disturbing your reading?"

"It's okay. I'm almost finished." She closed the Bible. She would read the last few verses later. Over the past three months, she'd almost completed the four Gospels. She was taking it slow, something else Courtney had encouraged her to do. If she attempted one of those complete-the-Bible-in-a-year plans, most of what she read would slip right past her.

She smiled at him. "As soon as breakfast is over, you can put me to work."

She didn't have to report in, but that didn't mean she'd be goofing off. Her new kitchen cabinets were arriving tomorrow afternoon. Cody had one of his guys lined up to remove the old ones today. He'd originally planned to schedule two workers, since excessive tugging, pulling and lifting weren't advised until his ribs had healed. But Erin had insisted on being the second demo person. She had no construction experience, but destroying a kitchen wasn't rocket science. Besides, working alongside Cody would be fun.

He put his steaming mug on the table and took the chair next to her. "I'll be glad to put you to work. A few days of this, though, and you'll be ready to get back to detectiving."

She grinned at his use of the made-up word. "Or I might decide I like construction better than detectiving and apply for a job with you." She drained the last of her coffee and put the empty mug on the table. "I'm hoping the others will make some progress on the case during my days off."

The units that had been dispatched to Cody's house in the early-morning hours two days ago had found nothing. Donovan's lead had gone nowhere, too. Detectives had talked with every contractor who ever bid on his jobs and were now working their way through the employees and subcontractors. Not a single one recognized the guy in Cody's composite. If there was a link between Donovan and their investigation, they hadn't found it.

Erin sighed. "Donovan has the most to lose if the project doesn't move forward, but he always has projects in the works. He says if this one doesn't go through, he's got five others waiting in the wings." She frowned.

"What he says is true, which kind of weakens the possibility of him being our suspect."

She deposited her coffee mug in the sink, then picked up her Bible and devotional book. Instead of taking them back to her bedroom, she left them on one of the living room end tables. Besides saving herself the trip down the hall, maybe Cody would get curious and check them out.

Cody called to her from the kitchen. "How about if I whip you up some scrambled eggs? I'll make Mimi and Opa's once they get up."

"Sounds good." She walked back into the dining room, where two flat, rectangular boxes stood against the wall. "I'll work on assembling those shelves we bought yesterday."

After she'd gotten home from work, they'd bought two plastic shelving units. She would use them to keep her dishes and food easily accessible while the kitchen was undergoing renovations.

Erin had just sat on the floor next to one of the boxes when Mimi entered the living room, walker in front of her, Opa behind her.

Cody looked in their direction. "Did our talking disturb you?"

"No. It was the smell of coffee that woke us up."

"There are still at least two more cups in the pot. And if scrambled eggs sound good, I'll have them ready in a few minutes."

At Mimi's acquiescence, Cody added four eggs to the bowl. While Erin sliced into the box with a utility knife and began removing components, Mimi sat at the table and Opa prepared their coffee.

When finished, he sat next to his wife. "Mimi and I are ready to head back home."

Erin stopped, one upright post held aloft. "Are you sure?"

"We were talking about it last night, after we went to bed. It's been a week and a half. We're ready."

Erin nodded, a lump forming in her throat. She'd enjoyed having her grandparents with her. Knowing they were just on the other side of the open door had put her mind at ease, and she wasn't ready to send them out on their own. But it wasn't her decision. She had to trust that Mimi and Opa knew what they were doing. And trust God to watch over them. The problem was, when it came to trust, she was a work in progress.

When breakfast was over, Mimi and Opa disappeared into the suite and came out a short time later with Opa wheeling their suitcases.

Erin looked at them long and hard. "Are you sure about this?"

They both nodded, and Opa grinned. "You guys live with a little too much excitement." He was probably only half joking.

Erin and Cody each took a bag from her grandfather and followed them to the front door. She hugged one, then the other. "Be careful driving."

Her grandfather shook his head. "Pumpkin, I've been driving back and forth to the hospital, then the rehab place, for more than two months."

But this was all the way to LaBelle. Of course, it was only forty-five minutes, a straight shot down Florida 80. And traffic was lighter.

"You'll have to get groceries. Except for condiments, I pretty well wiped out your refrigerator."

Cody put his hands on her shoulders. "You go with them."

"But—" She'd already done the math. She'd be hard-pressed to make the drive to LaBelle and still get home in time to unload the cabinets before Cody's guy got here at one o'clock.

Cody waved away her concerns as if he'd read her mind. "Go on. I'll unload the cabinets, and they'll be ready to remove by the time you get back."

She hesitated for another beat, then nodded. "Arm the security system."

"I will."

"And you'll feed Alcee her lunch if I'm not back in time?"

He smiled. "I always do."

Erin mouthed a silent *thank you*, hoping that he understood how much she appreciated him. Why had she ever given up a guy like Cody? What good had her freedom done her?

It had given her the ability to choose her own path. But what if the best life was the one she'd walked away from?

She stepped from the house with a sigh, then pulled out behind her grandparents. When they walked out of Winn-Dixie an hour and a half later, they had a full shopping cart with several bags lining the shelf beneath. Erin and Opa loaded them into the back of the Cube and drove the remaining seven miles to their park.

When Opa helped Mimi from the vehicle, she looked around, her face lit with joy. There really was no place like home. And Moss Landing was a beautiful park, right on the Caloosahatchee River, with street names like Shark, Porpoise, Dolphin and Bass Drives, and all the amenities one could want.

Instead of making her way up the ramp into the double-wide mobile home, Mimi met Opa and Erin at their vehicle's open back door.

Erin frowned at her. "What are you doing, Mimi?"

"Getting groceries. I'm fully capable." She grabbed a bag of produce and hung it over one of the walker arms, then added one to the other side. When she moved away, two more bags sat on the walker's seat.

Erin and Opa followed her, several bags looped over their arms. After one more trip, Erin had the rest of it inside. She helped them put everything away, then kissed them goodbye, with orders to call if they needed anything.

Once back in her SUV, she pulled her phone from her purse. She would text Cody and let him know she was on her way home. When she swiped the screen, she'd already missed a text from him. It was simple, an address, then CC. Probably short for *Cape Coral*.

But it was the three numbers that followed that put a knot of dread in her gut.

He'd ended the text with 911.

She checked the time stamp with her heart in her throat. More than fifteen minutes had passed since he'd sent the text.

With shaking fingers, she pulled up the keypad, ready to relay what she had to Dispatch. She had no idea what was significant about that location or what might be happening there.

But one thing she knew. Cody was in trouble.

God, please let someone get there in time.

Cody drove through the Friday lunchtime traffic, one hand on the wheel. The other was wrapped around his phone, currently pressed to his ear.

It was his business phone, the number that was on all his advertising and the one his customers used to reach him. It was Candy Hutchinson who'd called him this time, a sweet middle-aged lady, not the pushy type at all. But she'd phoned twenty minutes ago, pleading with him to come over so they could discuss some changes. And it had to be today. Now.

He'd promised to come right away, but every time he'd tried to end the call, she'd come up with something else, her tone even more urgent.

She was acting so out of character, he'd asked her if everything was all right. The assurances she'd given him weren't convincing at all. Something was off. So with his other hand, he'd grabbed his personal phone to send a quick text to Erin, then headed out. At the first red light, he pulled up the same text and forwarded it to Bobby.

He was walking into a trap, and he knew it. Someone was forcing Candy Hutchinson to make the call, trying to draw him out. Erin would have a fit. But what choice did he have? If he didn't cooperate, things could go badly for Candy.

The light ahead turned yellow, and he braked to a stop, again reaching for his personal phone. His neighbor Jack was another one who knew about the case. He'd be able to decipher his obscure text and call for help.

Cody held his thumb against the message, then selected Forward as Candy continued to babble. Now to select Jack's name from his contacts. Several seconds of silence passed before he realized Candy had asked him a question.

"I'm sorry. What was that?"

"I was asking about tile, the difference between porcelain, ceramic and marble. Do you recommend one over another?"

He touched Jack's name and pressed Send. A horn sounded behind him. Multitasking had never been his strong suit.

He returned the phone to the cup holder and surged forward, engine revving. Where were the cops when he needed them? For the past twenty minutes, he'd hoped to draw the attention of law enforcement by breaking a few traffic laws. If successful, rather than tipping off whoever was with Candy, he'd keep driving and likely have a tail three or four cruisers long by the time he rolled into the Hutchinsons' drive.

But he hadn't seen a single cop. And now the house was only three blocks away. He moved into the left turn lane and waited for the light to change. Had anyone gotten his text? He picked up the phone. Erin hadn't responded. Neither had Bobby or Jack.

Meanwhile, Candy continued to ramble. "Bill and I aren't in agreement on what we want. He wants to change the whole color scheme, materials and everything."

Cody dropped his personal phone back into the cup holder. He couldn't count on anyone seeing his message. Bobby and Jack were both at work, and Erin was en route from LaBelle. He needed to call 911.

But the killer was listening. Cody was sure. And the man was forcing Candy to keep him on the line so he couldn't call for help. Now time was running out.

"I'm about two minutes away. Let me go, and I'll be pulling in shortly."

"No, please don't hang up." Panic laced her tone. "This whole situation has me so upset."

The light changed, and Cody accelerated into the turn. How had his attacker linked the Hutchinsons to him? He and Leroy had gone by there a week and a half ago, but Erin had made sure they didn't pick up a tail. And since Leroy had driven, Cody had kept a constant eye on the traffic behind them, too.

It wasn't from raiding his home office, either. The Hutchinson job was the only one in progress, and he'd brought the file to Erin's when he'd collected the rest of his belongings.

As he moved down the Hutchinsons' street, his chest tightened. He should see emergency lights by now. But there was nothing.

He pulled into the drive and killed the engine. At every window, the blinds were drawn. The sight set off even more alarms.

Candy loved natural light. She'd told him so. The first thing she did every morning was open all the blinds in the front part of the house. He'd never seen any of them drawn other than the ones at the bedroom windows.

When he reached for the driver door, his gaze swept across the yard and settled on one of his signs— *Another quality project by Elbourne Construction*. His heart dropped. It hadn't been there when the three of them had visited previously. Bill must've removed it to mow and then put it back.

His signs were free advertising. This one was advertising he didn't want. Why hadn't he thought of it before? He'd made it easy for the killer to get to him.

He opened the driver door. "Candy, I'm here, so I'm hanging up now."

Maybe he could dial 911 before getting out of his truck, mumble a quick call for help and drop the phone into his pocket.

There was a slight pause before she responded. "Wait. Can you come in first?"

He hesitated. This was his last opportunity. No, he wouldn't put Candy in even greater danger. He picked up his personal phone, dialed 911, then dropped it back into the cup holder. Now that he'd arrived at his destination, they could trace his phone's location. Maybe the dispatcher would send help, even without him asking for it. He'd just have to stay alive until it arrived.

He stepped from the truck. A high-pitched whine sounded in the distance, definitely sirens. But that didn't mean they were for him.

He closed the truck door, listening as they drew closer. The vertical blinds at one of the living room windows parted, and something appeared in the opening. Cylindrical, such a dark shade of gray it was almost black.

The barrel of a pistol.

He dived sideways as a shot rang out, then rolled toward an oak tree. As he stood, a second shot sent splinters of bark spraying outward. He turned sideways and pressed his shoulder to the tree, hoping his body didn't overlap the medium-size trunk.

The sirens were so loud now, they set his teeth on edge. But he'd never heard anything so beautiful. Two police cars pulled into the drive, a third stopping at the edge of the road. The sirens died. A crash sounded from inside. Then another shot.

No, not Candy.

The first two officers jumped out, weapons drawn.

Cody remained behind the tree. "There's a gunman in the house."

The front door opened, and four weapons swung in

that direction. A second later Candy Hutchinson burst through as if she'd been shot out of a cannon.

"Hands in the air."

The command didn't register. She kept running, casting frantic glances back at the house.

Cody held up a hand. "She's the owner."

Her head swiveled in his direction, and relief flooded her features. She ran to him, plowing into him so hard she almost knocked him down.

"I'm so sorry." She threw her arms around his neck. "He said if I didn't get you over here, he was going to kill me."

Before he could respond, she spun to face the police. "He ran out the back. Blond hair, shoulder length. Mid to late thirties. Blue jeans and a yellow T-shirt with a fish on it, a Guy Harvey. A blue baseball cap, too."

The officers in the first two cars had already disappeared around the side of the house. One of the officers in front relayed the description over his radio. The other approached Candy.

"What happened?"

"The mail lady had just come. I walked to the box, and when I came back, a man jumped out of the bushes and forced his way in before I could get the door locked."

"Had you ever seen him before?"

"Never. He told me to get Cody over here."

The officer looked in his direction. "You're Cody?"

Cody nodded and brought the officer up to speed on everything that had happened. When Cody finished, he frowned. "He traced me to the Hutchinsons' through my sign, which was a pretty stupid oversight."

Candy continued. "Whatever the guy wanted with Cody, I'm sure it wasn't good. When he started shooting, I figured he wasn't going to leave either of us alive. I didn't have anything to lose, so I grabbed the vase from the table and brought it down over his head as hard as I could."

Cody's jaw dropped. That was the crash he'd heard. He didn't know Candy had it in her.

Candy pursed her lips. "His head was bleeding, and he was stumbling, but he was still on his feet. So I swung the brass lamp like a baseball bat, knocked the gun out of his hand and ran for the front door. By then, you guys had pulled into the drive, so he picked up the gun and ran toward the back."

If the officer was surprised at the spunk of this five-foot-two-inch lady, he didn't show it, just continued to take notes. "Can you describe the suspect, other than the clothing and hair?"

"Eight or nine inches taller than I am, somewhat stocky build. His face…" She looked at Cody and both officers, then frowned, apparently not finding what she was looking for.

"His face was a little longer than yours." She nodded at the younger officer. "And he had a beard and mustache."

"Do you think you could work with our artist to do a composite?"

"You betcha. He's had a gun pointed at me for the past half hour. I don't think I'll ever forget his face."

Cody gave her a wry smile. She made a much better witness than he did. Of course, she saw the guy for more than a second or two and wasn't drugged at the time.

He gasped and grabbed Candy's arm. "You and Bill have to get away from here." The killer had been relentless in trying to track him down so he couldn't identify him, and Candy had now seen his face.

The older officer nodded. "He's right. Do you have somewhere you can go until we catch this guy?"

"We have family. I need to call my husband. Can I do that now?"

"Sure."

A familiar SUV screeched to a halt in the street, and Erin jumped out. "I've been blowing up your phone for the past fifteen minutes. Why didn't you answer?" She hollered the words, her tone accusatory.

He bit back a defensive response. Erin's concern often came across as anger. The more worried she was, the angrier she appeared. It was one of her quirks. He could live with it.

He could even deal with her walls, because they seemed to be slowly crumbling. Her sharing with him what had happened in that remote cabin so many years ago was proof of that. But if they ever decided to move beyond friendship, she'd have to commit to a serious long-term relationship, and he'd have to risk someone walking away yet again. Neither scenario was likely in this lifetime.

He tapped his pocket. The phone was there. But that was his business cell. His personal one was sitting in the cup holder in his truck. He retrieved it and swiped the screen. There were numerous texts and missed calls from Erin, along with a missed call from Jack and a text from Bobby. Among the three of them, they'd probably kept Dispatch busy.

Cody turned back around to face Erin. But she wasn't watching him. Instead, she stood in profile, mouth agape. "Why did you put that up?"

"I put it up when I started the job, before the hurricane."

She planted her hands on her hips. "That sign was not here when we stopped last week. I would've noticed and told you to get rid of it."

"Bill took it down to mow and put it back up when he finished. But we were already gone."

Gradually, some of the panic fled her features, and she gave him a slow nod. Maybe she understood. But Erin wasn't the only one who had a hard time forgiving herself. He'd always been his worst critic, and he wasn't about to let himself off the hook that easily. His transgressions were piling up.

Convincing Pops to leave his home and come to Florida instead of making the move back home himself.

Not checking on Pops sooner and forcing him to leave well ahead of the storm.

Now carelessly leaving a sign in his customers' yard, leading a killer to their door.

Just one more mistake on an unending list.

NINE

Cody poured a cup of coffee, then doctored it with cream and sugar. The kitchen was as in need of work as it had been two days ago. The ugly harvest-gold appliances were still there. So were the green laminate countertops and the worn-out cabinets. After the excitement at the Hutchinsons' place, the remodeling had been put on hold until Monday.

He'd gotten about half of the items transferred from the cupboards to the plastic shelves before receiving the call from Candy. He'd take care of the rest tonight and be ready to start the demo in the morning.

Right now the house was quiet. Erin had left for a morning run with her neighbor and taken Alcee with her. She'd invited him to join them, but he'd refused. His sore body wouldn't handle forty minutes of pounding the pavement. Besides, he didn't want to crash Erin's girl time. He was upending her life enough.

He headed into the living room with his coffee. He'd promised Erin pancakes for breakfast, but if he wanted to serve them hot off the griddle, he'd have to wait thirty minutes to start them. In the meantime, he'd see if early Sunday morning programming offered anything interesting.

He sat on the couch and reached for the remote. It was sitting on the end table next to a Bible and the same book he'd noticed on Erin's nightstand. Bypassing the remote, he picked up the book and thumbed through it. Each of the pages had a date, but apparently, Erin wasn't following the recommended schedule, because her bookmark was inserted at the page marked March 7. He removed the bookmark, curious what she'd be reading that day.

The first sentence intrigued him. *Let Me help you through this day.* Given that the name of the book was *Jesus Calling*, he was probably supposed to read the words as if Jesus had spoken them. Was that what Erin did, relied on Jesus to help her get through the day? That didn't sound like her. If any woman could take care of herself, it was Erin.

While the first sentence caught his attention, the next two grabbed him by the throat. One said the challenges he was facing were too much to handle alone, and the next acknowledged the helplessness he felt in the events he was facing.

Yeah, he was feeling helpless. Who wouldn't in his circumstances? Driven from his home, the target of a foe who was always a step ahead of him. But he was dealing with it. He didn't need a crutch.

Without bothering to look up the scripture references at the bottom of each page, he moved through two more days, grumbling about those the same way he had the first. At the jiggle of the doorknob, he looked up with a gasp. The lock turned, the front door swung open and Alcee trotted into the room.

Cody grabbed the bookmark from the couch and stuffed it back between the pages. As he spun to return the book to its place, the corner hit the edge of the table. The book fell from his hand, hitting the hardwood floor with a thud. Erin stepped through the doorway, phone pressed to her ear. What was she doing back already?

He watched her gaze go from him to her book lying on the floor. Her brows lifted almost imperceptibly, but there wasn't any anger or annoyance. Probably because she was focused on her phone conversation.

He put the book back on the end table and hurried to the kitchen, Alcee following. Erin was such a private person. If she thought he was snooping through her things while she was away, she'd throw him out on the street. He measured some flour into a bowl and added the other dry ingredients. Maybe if he had breakfast ready for her when she finished her call, she'd go easy on him.

As he beat in the eggs and oil, Erin's voice drifted to him from the living room. That phone call was probably the reason she'd returned early from her run. Judging from her side of the conversation, there'd been some new developments in the case. One of her cases, anyway. He sometimes forgot his wasn't Lee County's only case.

While he worked, Alcee sat on the floor at his feet, occasionally pressing her side into his leg. She wasn't asking for anything. Erin had fed her before they'd left for their run, and since the dog hadn't been in that long, there was no way she had to go out. Now she just seemed to be guarding him against anything threatening. Though nothing dangerous was going to slither through the air vents or penetrate the glass behind the closed vertical blinds, it was a nice thought.

By the time Erin joined him in the kitchen, six pancakes sat on the electric griddle, undersides working their way to a golden brown. He cast her a glance over one shoulder. "News?"

"Yeah. Jordan McIntyre's girlfriend reported him missing this morning."

Cody's jaw dropped. Pops's neighbor to the right. "Maybe he witnessed something after all."

"That's an angle we're considering."

Cody slid the rubber spatula under the edge of one of the pancakes and peeked beneath. Perfect. After he'd flipped them all, he retrieved plates and glasses from the temporary shelving in the dining room.

Erin poured two glasses of orange juice and brought them to the table. "The residents in both houses said they evacuated before the storm. But maybe McIntyre learned something after the fact, and the killer is making sure he won't go to law enforcement with it."

She sat and drizzled some maple syrup over her pancakes. "His girlfriend was just about hysterical when she made the report. She insisted he didn't have any trips planned, or he'd have told her. They usually hang out at Dixie Roadhouse on Saturday nights, and he never showed to pick her up."

Cody waited while she bowed her head. Grace before meals was one of Erin's new habits, along with church attendance. And reading books like *Jesus Calling*.

She opened her eyes and cut into her pancakes. "It doesn't look good."

"Is his vehicle gone?"

She shook her head. "The Tacoma's still sitting in the

drive, so it looks like he disappeared from his house. We're there now, searching for clues. I told Danny to keep me posted." She took a long swig of her orange juice. "McIntyre seemed like a pretty nice guy. I'm hoping we don't find a body."

Cody frowned. "Knowing this guy's history with explosives, you might get your wish, just not in the way you hope."

The creep was determined to eliminate anyone who could identify him. At least Bill and Candy were gone. They'd cleared out before the sun set and headed to her sister's place in South Georgia. They didn't have to be told twice. The ordeal was probably going to leave Candy with some nightmares.

Cody's insides twisted. It was his fault. If he'd thought to remove his sign, the killer would never have connected him to the Hutchinsons. Fortunately, since this was his only job still in progress, there weren't any other signs out there.

He pushed the thought aside. He had other mistakes to atone for. "Sorry for messing with your things. I didn't mean to pry." Or maybe he did. If satisfying one's curiosity could be considered prying.

Her pancake-laden fork stopped halfway to her mouth. "Messing with my things?"

"Your book. I was planning to watch some TV while you were out. But instead of getting the remote, I picked up your book."

She gave him a relaxed smile. "It's not a diary. If I had a problem with you looking at it, I would've stashed it somewhere in my room. You're welcome to read it anytime."

She put the bite in her mouth and chewed slowly.

"I've found it helpful. So often, what I'm reading is just what I need at the time."

"I sort of figured that out."

"Several of the passages talk about trust. That doesn't come easy for me. Actually, it's a major struggle. Trusting God, trusting others. Even trusting myself."

He grinned. "I figured that out, too."

One side of her mouth lifted. "If you're reading *Jesus Calling*, you should know my Bible isn't off-limits, either."

"Now, that's pushing it."

When they'd finished breakfast, he took their empty plates to the sink. "I'll do these while you get ready for church."

"I'm not going."

He lifted his brows. Missing church without a good reason didn't seem like something Erin would do. "You're not staying home on account of me, are you?"

She shrugged, then followed him into the kitchen. When she started rinsing the plate he'd just washed, he frowned at her. The last thing he wanted was to keep her out of church. "Go ahead and go. Alcee won't let me out of her sight. When Candy called, I had to sneak out through the mother-in-law suite."

Her features drew into a scowl. "Sending that 911 text to me was smart, but you should never have left my house."

"And let Candy Hutchinson pay the price for something she had nothing to do with? I don't operate that way."

Her expression relaxed. "I know you don't."

The respect and admiration in her eyes sent a shot

of warmth through his chest. What she thought of him mattered.

"But if you'd like to attend church, I promise I'll stay put. I'm in good hands. Alcee seems to understand she's been charged with protecting me."

Erin shrugged. "I've got another two days of vacation. I figured I'd spend them with you." She grinned. "Besides, I don't feel like doing my hair and makeup."

Church or not, the hair and makeup weren't requirements. She looked great just like she was. Well, if she went to church, the yoga pants and T-shirt would have to go. But otherwise…

That long-ago summer in Punta Gorda, he'd seen her just one way—dressed in a tank, shorts and flip-flops, hair pulled into a ponytail, face clean and makeup free.

And he'd been completely smitten.

Now there were walls that hadn't been there before, and that carefree abandon had disappeared, but everything that had attracted him before was still there. If he wasn't careful, he was going to be right back in the same situation—hopelessly in love with a woman who wasn't willing to be anything more than a friend.

Was Erin fighting the same feelings he was? Did she feel the same draw, that longing for something deeper than friendship? If so, she kept it well hidden behind those walls she'd erected.

She finished placing the rinsed dishes in the rack. "My church livestreams its services. I figured we could watch from here."

Great. He wasn't leaving the house, but he was going to be stuck sitting through a church service. Oh, well, he could think of worse things than sitting next to Erin, a dog stretched across their legs.

Once they were finished with the dishes, Erin led him into the living room. "We've got thirty minutes till service time. What do you say we catch some news?"

She picked up the remote. A meteorologist stood in front of a map of the Gulf, pointing toward a large cone over the southern part of the state.

Cody sank onto the couch. "Are you kidding me? Three weeks after the last one?"

Erin smiled. "You weren't in Florida in the summer of 2004."

He narrowed his eyes. "You only told me about Charley."

"Charley's the one my grandparents and I went through. But two more hit the state from the other side. The three paths crossed within miles of each other in the middle of the state. Three major hurricanes within a six-week period." She shrugged. "So it's happened before."

Cody shook his head. "I guess I've had it easy. Until this season, we haven't had any bad ones since I've been here."

"We'll keep an eye on it. I've got hurricane shutters in the shed. They're easy to install. For the last storm, I put them up and took them down by myself." She frowned. "What about your place? If this thing's going to hit us, it won't be safe for you to go over there and do any kind of hurricane prep."

"I've got the electric rolling shutters. The remote is in my desk drawer. I could send my neighbor Jack in to do it."

"Better to have someone from the department do it. If the creep sees your neighbor go in, he'll know you've been in touch and might try to use him to get to you."

After letting Alcee out and back in again, Erin settled on the couch to watch her church service. Cody couldn't think of any way out of it without being a jerk, so he sat next to her.

It wasn't what he'd expected. Of course, he had only one experience to draw from. Years ago he'd visited a friend's church, a huge building in Chicago with vaulted ceilings, stained-glass windows and an organ with pipes spanning the height and width of the front loft.

He couldn't speak for his grandfather's church. Pops had invited him more than once. Cody had come up with an excuse every time. If he'd just given in, it would've meant so much to Pops. One more cause for regret.

He shut down the thoughts and focused on the television screen. Erin's church occupied what could have been a store at one time. Instead of a choir with its matching robes, three musicians and three singers stood in a row across the front platform, a drummer in the center. The songs weren't what he'd expected, either. Erin's church obviously didn't hold to the preconceived notion that music wasn't sacred unless written at least a hundred years ago.

But it was the sermon that caught him the most off guard. If he didn't know better, he'd think Erin had relayed the details of their conversation the other night to the preacher. Just like that devotional book. He was experiencing too much of that today.

When the message was over, one sentence stuck in his mind as if spelled out in neon. "You contribute nothing to your salvation except the sin that made it necessary." The pastor had attributed the quote to Jonathan Edwards, probably some famous preacher or something.

Whoever originally said it, the words disturbed him. He'd always felt religion was a crutch. He'd never been critical of those who needed it, but he didn't consider himself in that camp.

After the closing song, Erin killed the power on the remote. "What did you think?"

"It wasn't what I expected."

"In a good or bad way?"

"Neither. Just different."

"How did you like Pastor Mike?"

He lifted a brow. "Other than I think he's got your house bugged?"

Erin grinned. "No bugs. Not even any covert phone calls. But that's how God works. I can't tell you how many times I've felt like the preacher was talking directly to me."

He pursed his lips. "I'm not convinced. I mean, the concept of sin sounds a little antiquated, don't you think?"

"Depends on how you look at it. Granted, it's been around since Eve took the first bite of the fruit. But man hasn't changed much."

"I just don't see where all that's necessary."

"So you think you're perfect."

"No." Far from it. He'd made plenty of screwups. But they'd never been with intent to harm someone else, at least not since he was a troubled teen. "In the whole scheme of things, I think I'm all right. There are people a lot worse."

"It's not a scale, you know. Not in the way you're thinking. There's a standard, but it's not Hitler or even the guy next door."

He frowned. He'd had enough conversations with Erin to know what standard she was referring to. Jesus

Christ was perfect, which made Cody's attempts at being good enough pretty hopeless.

He pushed himself up from the couch. "What do you say we fix ourselves some lunch? Then we'll get the rest of the cabinets emptied."

By ten o'clock that night, they'd moved all the dishes and food stuff and relocated the refrigerator. They'd even made time for a long walk with Alcee in the ball park, since Erin's morning run had been cut short, and enjoyed a couple of movies.

Now they were both in their respective beds, and Alcee was on patrol, lying outside his door for short spurts, then padding down the hall to keep an eye on Erin.

The thoughts he'd kept at bay since the church service ended rushed back in. He'd shrugged off Erin's arguments. But lying alone in the dark, he couldn't dismiss them so easily.

The problem was, he'd spent most of his life trying to be good enough. If he'd been good enough, his mother would've loved him enough to stay.

If he'd been good enough, Erin would've finished college and come back to him.

If he'd been good enough, his ex-wife wouldn't have run off to find fulfillment with someone else.

He'd failed on all fronts. But maybe he didn't have to be good enough. Because someone else was. If he truly believed that, he wouldn't find the concept of Christianity to be so restrictive.

Instead, he'd find it freeing.

Erin opened the sliding glass door, and Alcee shot into the backyard. As Erin and Cody followed, the dog danced in front of them, dark eyes darting between Erin's face and her hands.

Usually, a trip out back meant playtime, especially if it happened right after she arrived home from her shift.

"Not tonight, girl."

She glanced at Cody. Beyond him, the sun sat perched against the treetops. "I've got the panels standing against the wall inside the shed."

Sunday and Monday there'd been little change in the storm's projected path. Most models showed it traveling due east across the southern tip of the state.

This morning that had started to change. By lunchtime, the huge mass of wind and rain was moving more northeast than east. Although another eastern turn was expected, no one agreed on when that would happen.

She slid the key into the shed's lock. Alcee still watched her, but her excitement had dwindled. Once this was over, Erin would give her some extra playtime.

She led Cody inside. "I know we're supposed to get just the northern edge of this, but I'd rather be safe than sorry."

He raised both hands. "You won't get any argument from me. After my recent experiences, I'm in support of any precautions you want to take."

"Good."

This one made her uneasy. It was as if something ominous was waiting to pounce the instant they let down their guards. Maybe the images of the emergency personnel pulling Cody's grandfather's unconscious form from the rubble were still too fresh in her mind. Or maybe it was knowing she was responsible for Cody's safety. Or maybe it was the combination of the storm and everything else that had been going on.

Whatever the reason, she was uneasy enough to go

to the trouble of reinstalling the shutters she'd removed after the last storm, even if it meant finishing in the dark via flashlight. Cody's home was already secured. Joe, aka Bobby, had gone in with Cody's key and lowered all of the shutters.

Mimi and Opa were safe, too. LaBelle was forty-five minutes inland from Fort Myers, but they'd gone to stay with some friends in Altamonte Springs, well north of the storm's projected path.

Erin grasped three of the fourteen-inch-wide metal panels and headed for the open door.

Cody followed her out with his own panels. "What about the hardware?"

"The bolts stay in the lower track, and I leave the wing nuts screwed onto them. So this is it."

Soon they had a good stack of panels leaning against the front of the house. After removing the wing nuts, Cody picked up a panel and slid it into the H-track over the first window, then secured it onto the bolts at the bottom.

He glanced at the western sky. All except the top edge of the sun had disappeared, and streaks of orange and pink stained the horizon. "I think we're going to be finishing this project via flashlight."

"You're right. But by daylight we'll probably be getting outer bands. I'd rather work in the dark than the rain." And she'd rather work with Cody than alone. Being alone had never bothered her. It beat spending her life tethered to someone who didn't make her happy. There was a third option—finding love with Mr. Right in one of those relationships that ended in happily-ever-after.

Except hers never did. So that left her with options one and two. Option one won, hands down.

But Cody's nearness over the past two weeks had her rethinking the appeal of being alone. There was something comfortable about having someone to cook and clean alongside her, someone to talk with and share the events of her day. Someone to hold her and chase away the remnants of a nightmare.

Someone to…love? No, she wouldn't go that far. She cared for him, always had. At one time she'd loved him. Things were different then. There'd been no need for protective barriers, because neither of them had had their ideals crushed and their souls bruised.

Erin removed the rest of the nuts and then frowned as Cody picked up another panel. "Are you sure you don't want me to lift those?"

"Broken bones heal in six weeks. Since I just passed three, I'm halfway there. Besides, these aren't that heavy. Not like using plywood."

Erin let him continue while she secured each panel with the wing nuts. "We had an interesting development in the McIntyre disappearance. Not sure if it means anything, but several of the guys that frequent Dixie said he showed up there alone the night before he disappeared and was trying to borrow money."

"Did anyone loan him the money?"

"Not that we know of. They claimed they didn't have the kind of money he was looking for. We're not talking beer money. We're talking several thousand dollars."

"Interesting."

Yeah, it was. They'd looked into his finances, and though he didn't have large sums of money in the bank, there weren't past-due loans or any debt, for that matter, other than his vehicle loan. And that was current. His girlfriend told investigators the same thing.

Cody frowned. "Maybe he borrowed money from some bad dudes, and they're calling in the loan. He might have disappeared on his own to keep from ending up in concrete boots at the bottom of Charlotte Harbor."

She nodded. Financial problems provided motive. Were the man's problems serious enough to prompt him to take down the apartment building to speed up the purchase of his property? Just how desperate was Jordan McIntyre?

As dusk gave way to darkness, they finished the front of the house, and Erin went in to retrieve a flashlight.

"Come on, girl. Let's go inside." The dog wouldn't run off. Even if she did, a simple command would bring her right back. But she and Cody had enough to do without the distraction of keeping up with Alcee.

They'd just finished the side when her cell phone rang. She pulled it out of her pocket and checked the screen, intending to let it go to voice mail. Instead, she frowned at a familiar number. "I've got to take this. It's my supervisor."

As she listened, Cody watched. She finished the call and pocketed the phone.

"I have to go in. McIntyre's girlfriend stopped by his place and surprised someone when she opened the front door. Her car's lights hadn't shut off yet. A guy ran out of the house, knocked her down and took off on foot. When he crossed through her headlight beams, she got a good look at him. Medium height and build, shoulder-length blond hair and a beard."

Cody's eyebrows dipped toward his nose. "What does our guy want with McIntyre?"

"I don't know." She handed him the wing nuts she held. "I'm sorry. I have to leave you."

"No problem. I'll finish this."

"Are you sure?"

"I'm positive. All we've got left is three windows in the back and what's on the other side. When I'm working inside the fence, Alcee can keep me company."

"The minute you're finished, get in the house and lock the doors."

He gave her a salute. "Yes, ma'am."

A few minutes later she was in her vehicle headed toward the station. As she turned onto Cleveland and left her neighborhood behind, her thoughts churned.

How were McIntyre and the guy who'd attacked Cody linked? Had McIntyre learned something? If so, he would have shared it with the police. Unless he was using it to blackmail someone.

McIntyre's girlfriend had lots of reasons for concern. There were too many scary scenarios. Whether a killer thought McIntyre knew more than he did, or McIntyre had stumbled onto knowledge about Cody's grandfather's murder, his life was in danger. And if he was stupid enough to get involved with loan sharks or attempt blackmail, that compounded the danger a hundredfold.

And now he'd disappeared.

Whatever the threat, things weren't likely to end well for Jordan McIntyre.

Cody lay in bed, eyes struggling to take in the minuscule amount of light that seeped into his room from Erin's at the end of the hall. She was home. He'd heard her come in, then gone right back to sleep.

Now he was wide-awake, an underlying tension flowing through his body. The moonlight that usually filtered in around the edges of the mini blinds wasn't there. With the hurricane shutters in place, darkness swallowed the window against the far wall.

Maybe Erin's practice of sleeping with night-lights wasn't a bad idea. Three was a little overkill, but one would've been nice. Because tonight something about the darkness disturbed him. It was making him feel… unsettled.

A whine intruded on the silence, followed by the click of claws against the hardwood floor. Alcee padded past his room toward Erin's, emitting another whine. What had the dog been doing in the living room, and what had her upset? Maybe his uneasiness didn't stem from the darkness.

Cody threw the covers aside and sprang to his feet, retrieving his phone with a quick sideways swipe. Whatever was going on, he needed to alert Erin.

It wasn't necessary. When he burst into her room, she was already sitting up. Alcee stood and put a paw in Erin's lap as Erin swung her silk-clad legs over the side of the bed. "What's going on?"

He shook his head. "I don't know. Alcee just came from the living room. I think she might have heard something."

Alcee turned from the bed and left the room, her repeated backward glances telling them to come with her. Erin snatched both her phone and her weapon from the nightstand and took off after the dog.

As Cody followed them into the living room, the uneasiness that had plagued him when he'd awoken bore down on him. With hurricane shutters covering every window, they were cut off from the world.

That could be good or bad. The killer couldn't see

them, even though Erin had turned on the hall light. But the shutters also kept them in the dark, ignorant of whatever threats lurked outside.

They'd just reached the living room when the dog erupted into frenzied barking, her eyes focused on the locked front door.

Erin raised her weapon. "Someone's out there. Call 911."

The next moment, the crack of splintering wood punctuated the sharp barks. The metal head of a sledge-hammer appeared through a jagged hole, then withdrew to strike again.

Alcee went nuts, charging back and forth in front of the door. Though Erin shouted at her to stand down and move away, none of the commands seemed to register. This scenario probably hadn't been a part of her training.

Erin grabbed the dog's collar with her free hand and pushed her in Cody's direction. "Quick! Get into the hall, and take Alcee with you."

"Come, Alcee." He moved away from the door, tugging the dog with him. "It's okay, girl."

By the time he reached the hall, four more hammer blows had opened a two-by-two hole in the heavy wooden door. With the locks undisturbed, the alarm hadn't been triggered yet.

Cody punched the three numbers into his phone and waited for the dispatcher. The killer had found him. With a few more strikes, he'd be inside the house.

Erin was ready. She stood next to him at the end of the hall, ready to shoot whoever came through the opening.

When the dispatcher answered, Cody relayed the

situation, his words tumbling over one another. The woman said she was dispatching police immediately.

"Please hurry. He's almost inside."

Cody clamped down on his lower lip. For the past several seconds everything had been quiet. They could escape through the back door, but running out blind didn't seem like a good idea. Had the assailant heard his 911 call and given up? Or was he waiting somewhere outside?

Cody had his answer right away. An object protruded through the opening, small and cylindrical. Like the barrel of a pistol or rifle. His heart leaped into his throat, and he jerked Alcee farther into the hall.

But something was off. The barrel had looked like a hard plastic. Why bring a toy gun? He peered around the corner in time to see a liquid stream arch through the opening. Several followed it, the angle shifting with each one to encompass the entire room. Erin fired three shots, but no grunts or shrieks indicated that any of them had found their target.

Within moments the stench of gasoline assaulted Cody's nostrils. Panic spiraled through him. The assailant planned to burn them alive inside the house. But even with the windows and sliding glass door covered, there were two other ways out.

He shouted one more command into the phone. "Send the fire department, too. He's soaking the living room with gasoline."

Cody slid the phone into the pocket of his gym shorts and grabbed Erin by the arm. "Come on." She'd want to stand her ground and protect her house. He understood. But it wasn't worth their lives. "We can escape out the back."

She gave a sharp nod. "Come, Alcee."

They'd just reached the back door when fire crackled behind them. Cody spun. A knotted bundle of cloth lay in the middle of the living room floor, engulfed in flames. Another missile followed, landing three or four feet away. Mini walls of fire erupted, flaming paths following the trails of gas. Within seconds the fire was moving across the living room rug.

He twisted the doorknob lock and threw the dead bolt while Erin grabbed the extinguisher from its holder two feet away. She pulled the pin and aimed a stream of foam at the base of the flames. The fire retreated as she swept left to right, then back again. Alcee stood at the door, her barking rapid and piercing. The alarm sounded, adding its shrill screech to the chaos.

Before Erin could make her third sweep, the stream sputtered and went out. She shook the extinguisher, then pressed the discharge lever again, eyes wide and panic filled. "It's empty."

"Don't worry about it." He pulled her toward the door. "We've got to get out of here."

He twisted the knob, but when he leaned into the door, it didn't budge. He gave it a harder shove. It still held fast.

When he looked back at Erin, the flames were moving forward with a vengeance, as if angry at her attempts to extinguish them. "The door's stuck."

Erin's eyes widened, and Alcee barked louder. They had to get out. Cody steeled himself for what he'd have to do. In spite of his broken ribs, he had a good seventy pounds on Erin.

He leaned back, then slammed his left shoulder into the door. The impact jarred his whole body, sending a bolt of pain through his right side. The door moved a half inch.

It wasn't stuck. Someone had wedged something against it. He cast another glance over his shoulder. Behind Erin, most of the living room was engulfed in flames. They danced across the couch and licked at the curtains. A haze hung in the air, and smoke rolled toward them.

He gave the door another try, with no better result than before. Perspiration soaked through his T-shirt, as much from fear and desperation as the wall of heat pressing into him. His nostrils burned, and his eyes watered. He inhaled, and his throat closed up midway through, inducing a coughing fit. After he recovered, he took several breaths through his damp T-shirt.

When he looked at Erin, she was filtering the smoky air through the neckline of her silk pajama top. Her eyes reflected his own desperation.

He attacked the door with renewed vigor, then shook his head. He couldn't do it. The only thing he'd accomplished was giving his body a beating. He looked frantically around him. The front door wasn't an option. Neither was the door to the mother-in-law suite. Reaching either one would involve a sprint through an inferno.

Desperation pressed down on him. "Is there any other way out? A pet door, anything?"

He knew the answer before he asked the question. He'd already looked the entire house over in preparation for the renovations. There was no other way out. Except...

Hope tumbled through him. "The attic." He'd noticed the framed opening in the hallway. "Do you know if the gable ends are vented?"

Her eyes widened, and a smile curved her lips. "Yes, they are." She grabbed his hand and pulled him toward the living room. "If we can get to the gable over my bedroom, we can kick out the grate and drop to the ground."

The flames had almost reached the dining room. The heat was intense, and he struggled to hold his eyes open against the stinging black smoke. Would his idea even work? The roof wasn't that steeply pitched. Erin was small enough to fit through the trusses, but he didn't know about himself. Then there was the challenge of climbing a wooden fold-down ladder carrying a full-grown German shepherd. In his current condition, he wasn't sure he could do it.

Erin scurried along the edge of the living room, back pressed against the wall, and Cody followed. Alcee held back, whining, flames reflected in her dark eyes.

"Come on, girl." Erin clapped her hands. "You can do it."

While Erin coaxed the dog, Cody reached up to pull the hinged panel down. He'd just finished unfolding the ladder and planting its end against the hardwood floor when Alcee shot around him and bounded up the wooden steps.

At his silent question, Erin smiled. "Ladders were part of her SAR training."

Erin made her way upward while a furry white face watched from above. She was barefoot. So was he. But moments taken to get dressed and retrieve shoes could cost them their lives.

Finally, it was Cody's turn. He released his shirt and held his breath. When he poked his head into the attic space, it was illuminated. A beam of light came from the back of Erin's cell phone.

He squatted on the step and reached below him. "I'm closing this back up. It'll help keep smoke out and buy us some extra time."

The hinges creaked as he folded the two bottom sections of the ladder against one another. His ribs again protested the abuse. He ignored the pain. He'd have time to recover later.

If they survived the night.

The access door creaked shut, and he looked around. Trusses lined up ahead of him, braces at uniform angles, held in place by metal fasteners. It would be a tight fit, but he was pretty sure he could make it, if there wasn't an air handler or anything obstructing his path.

Erin sent Alcee ahead, then began to make her way toward the end of the house. Cody followed, careful to keep his weight on the trusses. If Alcee stepped between them, onto the back of the drywall, the ceiling would hold her. Not so for him and Erin.

God, please help get us out of here. Would God even hear him? He was a pretty decent guy. He'd even watched a church service Sunday. But according to Erin, that wasn't what it took.

It wouldn't hurt, though, to add his prayers to the ones Erin was no doubt sending up.

Even though things didn't look half as hopeless as they had a few minutes earlier, they were still light-years away from being safe.

TEN

Erin made her way from truss to truss in a modified duck walk, the wood bruising the balls of her bare feet. As long as she kept her head down, she could pass through without having to lie down. She held her phone clutched in one hand, the beam from the flashlight app illuminating the way ahead of her. With her other hand, she moved her weapon forward, laying it between the next two trusses.

She should have grabbed the holster, but when she'd charged into the living room, ready to defend them, she hadn't anticipated having to crawl through the attic.

Alcee's training had prepared her well, and she'd navigated each two-foot span without a problem. Now she was waiting for them at the gable end. Beyond her, moonlight slanted through the rectangular vent in horizontal slivers.

Cody didn't have it as easy as her or her dog. He had to crawl from one truss to the next. Twice, Erin stopped to check on him, aiming the beam behind her. Though he was probably trying to hide it, she didn't miss his grimace of pain. Both times he told her to keep moving and not let him slow her and Alcee down.

He was right. Ominous creaks and groans vibrated through the wood beneath them. At any time the living room roof could collapse, sending heat, smoke and fire blasting through the attic space where they were. *God, please help us make it out of here.*

If anything happened to Cody or her dog, she'd never forgive herself. She should have replaced the fire extinguisher as soon as she moved in. She was going to, just hadn't gotten around to it yet. It hadn't been critical. The needle had still been in the green, a hairsbreadth away from the line separating it from the red *recharge* area, more than sufficient to extinguish a small kitchen fire or other minor mishap. She hadn't considered anything like this.

She stopped next to Alcee and ran a hand down her back. The dog's usual reward was a game of tug-of-war with her rope toy. Not this time. The toy was lying on the dining room table, where Cody had left it yesterday after playing with her.

The flames would've reached it by now. The whole table was likely ablaze, along with her new kitchen cabinets and everything she'd accumulated over the years. A wave of despair washed over her, so sudden and powerful it stole her breath.

She squared her shoulders. Her sole focus needed to be on getting Cody and Alcee to safety. She shone the light behind her. Cody was making progress but still had a good ten feet to go.

"Can you push out the grate?" His voice sounded strained.

She pressed against the metal. It felt solid, likely attached to the plywood with multiple screws. "I can't push it, but I can probably kick it out."

She squatted on her left leg and braced a shoulder against one of the trusses. After two hard kicks with her right foot, the grate dangled from one screw. She twisted it loose and tossed it to the ground. The opening was large enough to squeeze through, even for Cody. But escape would involve a ten-foot drop to the ground with no protection for their bare feet.

She turned off the light and scanned the area, weapon raised. The night was clear, the outer bands they expected still hours away. Moonlight spilled over the landscape. The hedge of sea grapes bordering her yard provided a good hiding place. She and Cody would be easy targets for someone waiting with a rifle.

But the killer wouldn't be expecting them to exit from the attic. He might even be gone, sure they'd be unable to escape. She listened for approaching emergency vehicles. What was taking so long?

She moved to the side and turned to Cody. "Squeeze through the opening, feet first."

"No way." His tone was adamant. "I'm not escaping until I know you're safe."

She heaved a sigh. They were losing precious seconds arguing. "I'm covering you. At the first sign of attack, I'll shoot." In all her years in law enforcement, she'd never had to kill anyone. But if it came to that, she'd do it without hesitation.

She pushed him toward the opening. "As soon as you're on the ground, I'll tell Alcee to jump. I need you to catch her. I don't know that I can handle sixty-five pounds falling through the air."

Cody stared her down for another second or two, eyes hard and jaw tight. Jumping to safety while she was still in danger clearly went against every protective instinct he possessed.

She gave him another nudge. "Don't worry. Alcee will be right behind you. And I'll be behind her."

The emotions skittering across his face collided in his eyes. The air between them was heavy with tension. Suddenly, he grabbed her by the shoulders. Before she knew what was coming, he pressed his mouth to hers in a hard, desperate kiss. Warmth exploded inside her, searing her mind and stealing the strength from her limbs.

All too soon he pulled away, waiting another second to release her. If he hadn't given her that moment to recover, she'd have fallen between the trusses in an undignified blob. The warmth inside was gone, replaced by longing so intense it was painful.

She struggled to set her world back on its axis while Cody backed into the opening. Lifting her weapon, she kept watch through the small spaces over his shoulders. He'd just put one foot through when a voice came from somewhere outside.

"Don't go any farther, or I'll shoot."

She stiffened at the voice with its heavy Northeast accent, the same Cody had described the day of his rescue. He jerked away from the opening, and Erin peered around the edge of the wall.

Everything was still. She fixed her gaze on the hedge, straining to see something. There was no hint of movement, no variations in texture or color amid the large rounded leaves.

"The police are already onto you." The confidence she injected into her tone masked the fear coursing through her. "Cody isn't the only witness. The woman you held at gunpoint for a half hour gave the police a pretty detailed description."

There was McIntyre, too. Chances were good he'd seen something, and the killer knew it.

"You already have one murder to answer for."

Well, two. Each day that passed, McIntyre was less likely to be found alive.

A distant wail traveled on the quiet night air. Behind her, Cody spoke in hushed tones. She cast a glance over her shoulder. He held his phone pressed to his ear.

"Send the police to the north side of the house." Urgency filled his tone, in spite of the softness of his words. "We're in the attic, and there's a shooter on the ground."

The emergency vehicles grew closer.

"Hear that?" Erin projected the words through the opening while Cody's soft conversation with Dispatch continued. "The police are on their way. Give it up. If you turn yourself in now, you've got a chance of getting off. You didn't mean to kill anyone. The courts will take that into account."

"The building was supposed to be empty."

She jerked her gaze in the direction of the voice. He was definitely behind the hedge. If she wasn't too far off on the angle, he was at about eleven o'clock. She needed to try to keep him talking. "I know. They'll understand that."

"No, they won't. Murder is murder. Cody saw me, and it's just a matter of time until he figures it out."

Figures it out? What was he talking about?

Before she had a chance to ponder further, there was a large crash, and the house shivered. Moments later a blast of heat and smoke whooshed past them and out the opening in the gable. A section of roof had caved in.

She cast a panicked glance over her shoulder. The flames had reached the attic and were charging toward them.

"Go, now!" She gave Cody another push. "Stay low so I've got a clear shot."

The sirens were closer now. She could hear them over the roar of the fire. But help wouldn't arrive in time. The flames were advancing too quickly.

Cody lay facedown and shimmied backward while Erin held her position beside him in a deep squat. She peered out the top left-hand corner of the opening, right arm extended, weapon clutched in that hand. How would she be able to hit anything in such an awkward position?

Smoke billowed around her, stinging her eyes and searing her throat. She waved a hand in front of her face, but more rolled in to obstruct her view.

God, help me do what I must to protect Cody and Alcee.

Cody squeezed into the opening, legs dangling down the outside wall. As he pushed his torso through, Erin repositioned herself to steady her aim with her left hand. For a fraction of a second, Cody hung suspended. Then he released his grip to fall to the ground. The same moment, the hedge moved. The crack of a gunshot followed, the simultaneous muzzle flash vivid in the darkness.

Erin fired three rounds. A cry came from the hedge—half grunt, half muffled shriek.

"Cody!" She'd wounded the shooter. But had he hit Cody?

"I'm okay."

Her breath came out in a rush. The emergency vehicles were closer now, their high-pitched wails filling the night. Tears streamed down her face, and several deep coughs stole her air. When she cast a glance over her shoulder, flames licked at the wood less than ten feet behind her.

"I'm sending Alcee down."

She wiped away her tears, made worse by the coughing fit, then again fixed her gaze on the hedge. Cody straightened and stepped a couple of feet away from the house, arms extended upward. Without relaxing her aim, she commanded Alcee to go.

As Alcee jumped, another shot rang out, and Erin fired again. Cody released a grunt as the dog landed in his arms.

"I've got her. We're good."

The sirens were ear piercing now, coming from right in front of the house. They fell silent, and only the roar of the fire surrounded her.

She gave in to another coughing fit, then shouted down at Cody, her voice raspy. "You and Alcee get to safety." Safety would be out front, where officers were likely exiting their cruisers, weapons drawn.

She held her breath against the smoke streaming past her and prepared to back her body into the opening.

A crash shook the house, and everything around her shuddered. A blast of heat slammed into her, and a ball of fire shot toward her at light speed.

She spun to face the opening, curled into a squat and leaped into the smoke-filled darkness.

Cody lay in the grass on his back, Erin on top of him. For several long moments he couldn't breathe. Pain stabbed through his rib cage, and his lungs were paralyzed.

He'd put Alcee behind the air-conditioning unit to shield her from the shooter's view. Then instead of obeying Erin's command to get to safety, he'd moved into position to help lower her to the ground.

His plans hadn't gone as he'd hoped. A series of cracks had shaken the house, and flames had shot twenty feet into the sky over where the living room roof had been. Instead of dropping gently to the ground, she'd jumped, and he'd tried to catch her.

Alcee bounded toward where they lay. After sniffing his face, she turned her attention to Erin and nudged her shoulder with her nose.

Erin rolled off him and tried to pull him to his feet. "Come on. Let's get to safety."

He nodded, unable to do anything else. The shots had stopped as soon as the police pulled up in front. Two officers had already disappeared behind the hedge to pursue the suspect on foot.

Finally, the vise around Cody's chest released. He sucked in a constricted breath, then followed it with several painful coughs.

Erin cast a nervous glance toward the hedge. "Can you walk?"

"I think so." Or maybe he was being overly optimistic.

He fought his way upright and stumbled with her into the front yard, Alcee following. The streetlamp near her property line spilled its light over them. More emergency vehicles approached, their sirens growing louder. Probably fire and ambulance.

Deep, painful coughs overtook him. He stood bent at the waist, hands on his knees. Erin was having the same struggle. They'd both inhaled too much smoke.

When she recovered, she wiped her eyes. "Are you okay? I wasn't sure back there."

He nodded. "You just knocked the breath out of me."

"Thanks for breaking my fall. But I told you to get to safety, not stand there waiting to be shot at again."

Cody patted the dog's hip. "I hid Alcee behind the AC unit so she wouldn't be shot, but I told you before. I wouldn't escape until I knew you were safe."

The scolding left her eyes, and an uncharacteristic tenderness moved in. That kiss he'd given her in the attic was a mistake. It was clear now that they were both safely on the ground. But that didn't stop him from wanting to do it again.

A fire truck arrived, an ambulance not far behind it. One firefighter rushed toward them while the other unwound the hose to attach to the hydrant in front of the house next door.

"Is everyone out?"

"Yes. She and I are it." And Alcee. If the attack had happened a few days earlier, Opa and Mimi would've been there. The outcome might have been different with two older people in tow. Erin would say they owed that detail to the hand of God. So would Bobby. Cody wasn't sure. But just in case, he whispered his own prayer of thanks.

Two paramedics approached. Erin made it halfway through an inhalation before a cough took over again. Knowing Erin, she'd downplay her injuries. Cody wouldn't let her.

"She needs to be treated for smoke inhalation."

Erin lifted a hand. "I'll be all right."

Her voice was several pitches lower than usual, deep and raspy. His was, too.

"You inhaled a lot of smoke." He turned to the paramedics. "She was the last one out of the house."

As soon as the words left his mouth, he winced. He

shouldn't have escaped first, no matter how adamant she'd been.

One of the paramedics put a hand on his shoulder. "Let's get you both checked out."

Cody let him lead them to the ambulance, where they both sat on the back. Erin's condition seemed worse than his, but he was having trouble drawing a full breath. Whether from the smoke, the broken ribs or Erin body-slamming him, he wasn't sure.

A second ambulance arrived, its siren falling silent. A short distance away the hedge rustled, and Cody tensed. But there was no threat. Two police officers stepped into the yard, a struggling man between them. One officer carried a rifle in his free hand, a cloth wrapping the barrel where he held it.

A blond wig sat cockeyed on the suspect's head, skewed a good forty-five degrees to the left. Curls tumbled past his shoulder on that side, the same curls they'd seen at the hospital. Was the beard fake, too?

Cody squinted at the man's clothes in the streetlamp's glow and the light cast by the semicircle moon. A large wet spot marked the right shoulder of the T-shirt, making the dark fabric even darker. Blood. Erin had hit him. He'd heard the man cry out. That shot had likely saved their lives. With a bullet in his shoulder, the man's next shots had gone wild.

The man turned, and the wig slipped another forty-five degrees before falling to the ground.

Erin gasped. "Jordan McIntyre? Why?"

He didn't respond. Cody didn't expect him to. But he hoped they'd eventually have some answers. It wouldn't bring Pops back or make up for everything he'd been through, but it might bring some closure.

While the paramedics worked on him and Erin, Alcee sat and watched, dark eyes alert. Other emergency personnel treated McIntyre, and firefighters continued to shoot powerful streams of water onto the flames. Soon, they'd have the fire put out. Maybe part of the mother-in-law apartment and Erin's bedroom and bathroom would be salvageable. He didn't hold out hope for anything else.

He looked over at Erin as a blood pressure cuff tightened on her arm. "I'm sorry about your house."

She gave him a sad smile. "We're safe, and that's what matters. Things can be replaced. People can't."

How well he knew that. He released a sigh. "It's over."

Erin glanced at the other ambulance. "I didn't see that coming. McIntyre grew up in Florida. The Northeast accent he used was as fake as the hair and beard." She took a rapid, shallow breath. "But it was him in every attack. And who his girlfriend surprised at his house last night."

Cody gave her a wry smile. "You wondered what connection there was between the blond guy and McIntyre. There's your answer."

A bathrobe-clad woman stepped off the porch next door and approached. "Are you guys okay?"

Erin nodded. "We're okay, but they're taking us to the hospital to check us out. And I'm worried about Alcee. I'm sure she inhaled as much smoke as we did."

"No problem. I'll get dressed and take her to the emergency clinic."

"Thank you. Have them call me for my credit card information."

The woman dropped to one knee. "Come here, girl."

Alcee went right to her. Cody had met the woman previously. According to Erin, she'd cared for the dog before he and Erin's grandparents moved in. The neighbor headed back to her house with Alcee in tow, removing an excuse Erin would've used for not getting checked out.

At the paramedic's request, Cody opened his mouth for him to look at his throat. Erin was undergoing the same assessments, and judging from the comments he overheard, the man wasn't happy with what he was seeing. Something about soot in airway passages, red and irritated eyes and rapid breathing.

The paramedic tending Erin stepped back. "We're hooking *you* up to oxygen right away, but we need to take you both in for observation. You might think you're okay now, but things can worsen in a hurry as swelling and mucus increase. Breathing isn't something to play around with."

Cody nodded. "Take her. I'll follow."

Erin nailed him with a stern glare. "Oh, no, you don't. If I'm going to the hospital, you are, too."

He held up both hands in surrender. "I'm going, just not in an ambulance. When this is over, we're going to need a ride home."

"I've got friends. Coworkers, too. Any number of them will be willing to pick us up."

"No need for that. I'm perfectly capable of driving." He wanted to be able to get out of there as soon as the doctor released him. He hated hospitals, at least when he was the patient.

She narrowed her eyes. "If I find out you bailed, I'll hunt you down and bring you in myself. In handcuffs, if I have to."

"Yes, ma'am. I'll be right behind the ambulance and won't leave until I get a clean bill of health. Now get on that gurney and let them get some oxygen in you."

"When did you get so bossy?"

He left the question unanswered. The fire was out, and the firemen were putting away their equipment. Wisps of smoke rose from a collapsed and smoldering center, capped by the two ends still standing.

An investigator would likely make contact with Erin tomorrow. She'd also need to report the incident to her insurance company. Then would come all the work of filing a claim, obtaining estimates and getting her home rebuilt.

But the first priority was taking care of her medical needs. His, too. Because if he skipped getting checked out, she'd do just what she threatened.

Soon, everything would go back to normal. He'd return home, and there'd be no reason for him and Erin to have contact beyond what they wanted. He didn't know what Erin wanted, but he knew his own desires. In a perfect world, he'd keep Erin by his side forever.

But it wasn't a perfect world. It was a world where plans changed on a whim and hearts got so badly broken they never fully healed.

The first time Erin left him, he'd been devastated. If he gave his heart to her and she walked away a second time, it would destroy him.

It was a risk he wasn't willing to take.

The television broadcast its morning programming into an otherwise silent room. Erin lay in the bed, staring out the tall, narrow window, a small hose feeding oxygen into her nose.

Over the past few hours the rain had come and gone. The storm did make that projected eastward turn, so the Fort Myers area had been spared the worst. She was one of a handful of people in her neighborhood who'd boarded windows to protect their homes. Then she'd lost hers to a fire.

She picked up her phone from the bedside table. No missed calls or texts. Cody had texted her at seven o'clock. After being kept awake by a nasty cough for several hours, she'd finally fallen into a fitful sleep and hadn't woken up for the notification. Her return text at eight fifteen had gone unanswered so far. Now it was almost ten.

She'd already called her insurance company and, between coughing fits, told the representative what had happened. They'd promised to send an adjuster to survey the damage later that day.

She'd also taken a call from a panicked Courtney, who'd thought she might have heard sirens over the sounds of her white noise machine but had missed the other commotion. Courtney hadn't seen the condition of the house until she'd left for work that morning.

The familiar tickle in Erin's throat started again, and she leaned forward as more deep coughs overtook her body. When the spell passed, she plopped back against the bed. Her chest hurt and her abdominal muscles felt as if she'd completed a couple hundred sit-ups.

Her head was killing her, too. Whether from the smoke she'd inhaled or all the coughing she'd done, she wasn't sure. The mucus was forming faster than she could get rid of it. Her hopes of being discharged today were growing dimmer by the hour.

She shifted her gaze back to the window. Maybe she

should try calling Cody. No, if his night had gone like hers, he was probably sleeping. She was just bored; no reason to disturb his rest.

Okay, maybe it was more than boredom. She was restless, confused. They were at a crossroads, and she had no idea where she stood.

Over the past few weeks they'd fallen into an easy camaraderie. She'd hoped that could continue, that they'd maintain a friendship. She'd been sure that was all she wanted.

Then he'd kissed her. Just thinking about it sent her pulse into overdrive. That kiss had to have meant something. Or maybe it had just been an impulsive response to emotional stress, the uncertainty of not knowing whether they'd survive the night.

Footsteps sounded outside her room. She turned away from the window, expecting a nurse. Instead, Cody approached wearing a warm smile and a pair of shorts and T-shirt she'd never seen before. A plastic bag dangled from one hand. In his other hand, he held two more bags.

Her stomach did a backflip. Then she narrowed her eyes. "Why aren't you in a hospital gown?"

He'd texted her to see how she was doing. He hadn't mentioned anything about his own treatment. If he'd reneged on his promise to get checked out, she was going to flog him.

"I've been discharged. I was asleep when you texted me back, didn't wake up till the doctor came in. He said he was releasing me later this morning, so I figured I'd come in person and surprise you instead of sending a text." He pulled a pair of sneakers from one of the bags and plopped them on the floor.

"You've got my tennis shoes."

"Yeah." He pulled the chair up beside the bed. "After they loaded you in the ambulance, I asked the firemen if I could grab my keys and wallet and shoes since I was driving myself to the hospital. The fire was completely out at that point, and anything that was going to fall had already fallen. But they still wouldn't let me go inside. Rather than leaving me stranded, though, one offered to get what I needed. While he was at it, I asked him if he could grab some shoes for you, too."

"Thanks."

"There's more. Bobby called right after the doctor left. When I told him what had happened, he asked if there was anything he could do. I asked him to swing by Walmart and pick us each up a change of clothes." He pulled a T-shirt and some exercise pants out of the second bag. "I hope I got your size close. At least spandex is pretty forgiving."

She held the items up. "It looks like you did pretty well."

"I have one more surprise for you." He reached into the last bag and pulled out her devotional book.

Her mouth dropped. "But how…?" The book had been in the living room. There was no way it survived the fire.

"I sent Bobby on one other errand. I asked him to go by the Christian bookstore and pick up two copies of *Jesus Calling.*"

"Two?"

"One for each of us. Since I'm going home, it'll be a little hard for us to share."

Erin couldn't stop the grin that spread across her face. "And the Bible?"

"I haven't gotten one yet. But I did find a free app for my phone. Bobby said I should start in the Book of John."

"Courtney said the same thing. Good advice." She paused. "So what brought this about?"

"I had trouble sleeping last night. I couldn't stop thinking about how close I came to dying. That kept going through my mind, along with bits of your pastor's message and our conversation afterward, as well as some of the things I've been reading in your book. I finally told God that my life is a mess, but if He wants it, it's His."

She reached out and squeezed his hand. "You won't regret it." She certainly hadn't.

He sat back in the chair. "When are they releasing you?"

"Not today. I'm still coughing up a lot of junk. They're doing another chest X-ray this afternoon, making sure no delayed lung injury shows up."

His brows drew together over eyes filled with concern. "Are you having shortness of breath?"

"A little. That's another thing they're concerned about."

"When they do let you out, you're welcome to stay with me until your house is livable again." He gave her a crooked smile. "I'll get to return some of that Southern hospitality."

"Thanks for the offer, but Courtney beat you to it."

"Already?"

"I got a call from her right after I talked to the insurance company. She was leaving for work, saw my car still sitting in the drive and the house half destroyed." She gave him a wry smile. "It took me a while to calm her down."

Two soft raps sounded on the doorjamb, and Erin

looked past Cody to where a Lee County detective stood just inside the room.

"Jeff, come on in."

He approached, shaking his head and making clucking sounds of disapproval. "You're back on duty one day after a four-day vacation, and now this. You'll do anything to finagle more time off."

She laughed. As she made introductions, Cody stood and offered the detective his chair, taking the one farther away. Erin filled Jeff in on what had happened inside the house from the time Cody showed up in her bedroom doorway until she'd leaped from the attic.

Jeff released a whistle. "Scary."

Yeah. It would probably give her fodder for some pretty serious nightmares. Not that she didn't have enough already.

But they hadn't come last night. Her cough hadn't allowed her to get into REM sleep. Once life got back to normal, she'd be adding fire and the thought of being burned alive to the other terrors that tormented her sleep.

Or maybe, if she truly trusted God for the healing she craved, she'd defeat all of them.

Jeff intertwined his fingers over his abdomen. "We finally got the toxicology report back, not that it matters at this point. The soup was positive for arsenic."

Though Erin had expected as much, the news was still jarring. She shook her head. "I still can't believe Jordan McIntyre was the one behind all of this. I'm usually a good judge of character. I don't suppose anyone has gotten him to talk."

"That's another reason I stopped by, other than to

check on you. Those background checks we did turned up some interesting things."

"What kind of things?"

"He did a short stint in the military and was dishonorably discharged fifteen years ago."

"What was his assignment?"

"He worked on a demolition crew."

She raised her brows. "As in blowing things up?"

He nodded. "That was part of it. Since his discharge, he's done a variety of construction-type jobs."

"That fits with what he told me."

"Part of it. Your report says he came from Wisconsin."

"That's what he told me."

"He did come from Wisconsin…by way of New York and New Jersey."

She frowned. "Why didn't he mention those states? Were his stays there brief?"

"A total of almost six years. While in the Northeast, he worked for three different demolition companies. Apparently, when he left, he took some souvenirs."

Her eyes widened. "No wonder he didn't mention New York and New Jersey."

He nodded. "It was safe to tell you about Wisconsin, because he held carpentry jobs there. Demolition companies in his work history would've raised too many red flags."

"What about the Camry? McIntyre drives a red Tacoma, and that's the only vehicle titled to him. We checked."

"He got the Camry a while back, never transferred the tag. He rents warehouse storage space in Cape Coral where he keeps it stashed."

Erin shook her head. "I still don't understand why

he did it. He had a good job, no money problems." Or so they'd thought until learning he'd hit his friends up for money.

"There's where you're wrong. Once we told him everything we'd learned, he came clean with the rest of it. Turns out he has a gambling problem and got in over his head. He'd been stringing the guys along for a few months. They finally threatened a slow and painful death if he didn't pay up."

Erin nodded. The last of their questions had been answered. After saying his goodbyes and wishing Erin well, Jeff left the room.

Cody took the chair he'd vacated. "It's hard to believe it's finally over."

"I know."

Ever since escaping the house, she'd been waiting for that sense of relief to settle in. It was there, but too many other emotions overshadowed it.

Now that the danger was over, Cody would return to his own home. As friends, they'd occasionally get together. But with no real excuse to see each other, those times would grow further and further apart, until they lost touch completely. She'd had more than one friendship disintegrate that way. Sometimes she regretted not having a social-media presence. It at least kept people loosely connected.

Somehow, she'd make sure she didn't lose contact with Cody. He'd become an important part of her life and she wasn't ready to let him go.

Who was she kidding? What she felt went way deeper than that. She didn't just care for him. She'd fallen in love with him. Judging from everything he'd poured into that kiss, he had to be feeling at least some of what she was.

"I'll be heading home today, getting back to doing estimates and meeting with customers without a baby-sitter." His words cut across her thoughts, so practical and unemotional compared to the path hers had taken. "I'd leave you your spare key, but if you're going to have me do the repair work, you might want me to hang on to it."

"That would be a good idea."

"Would you like me to pick up Alcee and take her home with me till you get out of here?"

"That would be great."

Their interactions had become stiff. What was he feeling? She had to know.

"You kissed me in the attic."

His gaze dipped to the floor. "I'm sorry. I didn't mean it. I was afraid we weren't going to make it out of there alive." He met her eyes. "It won't happen again."

"No problem." She forced the words past a lump in her throat.

The kiss had meant nothing. It was just what she'd thought but hoped against—an impulsive reaction in an emotional moment.

At one time he'd been ready to commit to forever. She'd wanted the freedom to experience life. Over the past twelve years she'd learned adulthood wasn't all it was cracked up to be. Neither was freedom.

She'd removed the rose-colored glasses and found what she really wanted had been right in front of her.

But that window of opportunity had closed.

ELEVEN

Cody strolled next to Erin, the Punta Gorda Harbor-walk stretching before them. Peace River lay to their left, reflecting a blue sky dotted by a handful of clouds. A light breeze negated the September heat and humidity.

Erin smiled up at him. "Thank you for dinner." They'd left Hurricane Charley's Raw Bar and Grill a few minutes ago and would soon cross under the southbound Tamiami Trail bridge. "Alcee says thanks, too. She's gotten spoiled with all this fine dining."

"No problem." He gave Erin a smile of his own. "I owe you at least two more thank-you-for-saving-my-life dinners. Or is it three? It's happened so many times, I've lost count."

A week had passed since Erin had been released from the hospital. They'd kept her a day and a half longer than they had him. Now they were both back at work. He didn't know about her workload, but between finishing the Hutchinson addition and continuing to provide estimates, he'd been slammed. They'd talked but had seen each other only once.

Sunday morning he'd surprised her by sliding into

the pew next to her. He'd gotten to meet Pastor Mike in person, along with several of the other church members. Now he had a new activity in his schedule—weekly church attendance. He hoped it would be with Erin. If not, he'd try Pops's church. If Pops could see him now, he'd be smiling.

A box truck roared closer as they stepped into the shade of the overpass. Cody waited for it to move by, his smile fading. "I'm afraid I owe you guys more than a few dinners. You lost your house because of me." He frowned. "But now that it's over, I'll get my debt paid eventually."

She gave him a little push. "There's no debt. None of it was your fault. But I'm sure if Alcee could talk, she'd tell you to keep the dinners coming."

He grinned. "I'm sure she would."

Even though he hadn't seen much of Erin, she'd never left his thoughts. He missed her, more than he ever imagined he would. Two nights ago he'd clicked on the TV, hoping to dispel his loneliness with some evening sitcoms, and found they made a poor substitute for the nearness of one amazing woman and her dog.

So yesterday he'd come to a decision, made a trip to the Punta Gorda Post Office, then called Erin to set up today's outing. Now he needed to work up the courage to continue with his plan.

The Harborwalk made a couple of bends, and the northbound Tamiami Trail bridge stood in front of them. Soon, they'd be back at Laishley Park, where he'd left his truck.

And where he'd hidden a key.

His stomach rolled over, and his palms grew moist. When it came to reading women, he wasn't always the brightest bulb in the pack. Erin had brought up the kiss he'd given her the night of the fire, and he'd been sure a reprimand was coming, at least an explanation of why she thought it was a mistake. So he'd beaten her to it, rushing ahead to assure her the kiss had meant nothing when it had shaken his world.

But she hadn't looked relieved. Instead, he'd seen disappointment in her eyes, noticed how her face had fallen, the almost imperceptible way her shoulders had curled forward. He'd hurt her.

Now he was going to take those words back. Maybe. What if he'd read her wrong? What if he'd seen relief instead of disappointment? It wouldn't be the first time he'd been clueless about a woman's thoughts and feelings.

Erin cast him a sideways glance. "Are you in a hurry to get home?"

"No. Why?"

She shrugged. "I was thinking about watching the sunset."

"Sure."

A lot of eagerness came through in his tone. He didn't care. All evening he'd tried to read her mannerisms, to search out meaning behind her words, anything that might hint at where he stood with her. She'd given him nothing. How had he expected anything else? He'd kissed her, then told her it meant nothing.

But now she wanted to spend more time with him doing something nostalgic. How many times had they enjoyed the sunset from one of the park benches overlooking the water while Pops fished nearby? It had to be a good sign, right?

When they took a seat a few minutes later, Alcee

plopped down at their feet. The first streaks of orange already stained the western sky, the bridge in the foreground. As the sun sank lower, Cody lifted his arm to let it rest on the back of the bench.

Erin didn't lean into him, but she didn't stiffen or pull away, either. Another good sign. Or maybe he was grasping at straws.

She released a soft sigh. "I love the sunsets here."

"Me, too."

There was something special about watching the sun set over water. But what had always made the Laishley Park sunsets special was sharing them with Erin.

He bent his arm to encircle her shoulders. Now she did lean into him, and he gave her a squeeze.

Okay. This was it. He was going to do it.

The colors deepened, and the sun disappeared into the horizon. Behind them, palm fronds rustled in the gentle breeze, and distant voices drifted to them. Dusk settled in.

Cody rose and held out a hand. "Let's walk."

She grinned up at him. "The two-mile hike we took earlier wasn't enough for you?"

Yeah, they'd covered a good percentage of the two-and-a-half-mile Harborwalk, heading toward the Village Fish Market on its southwest end, then stopping by Hurricane Charley's on their way back.

"We've got one quick visit to make."

She put her hand in his, and he helped her to her feet, ignoring the raised eyebrow and head tilt. When he intertwined his fingers with hers, she didn't seem to mind.

They continued hand in hand, past streetlamps and another bench before the sidewalk veered right. Soon they stood in front of the Hurricane Charley memorial with its sundial and two palm trees.

"This is where we're going?" She looked up at him. There was a lot of curiosity in her gaze. But something else, too. Anticipation? Excitement?

"Have you ever checked the palm fronds?"

"Should I have?"

"Maybe."

She narrowed her eyes. "What did you do?"

"Something I should have done eight years ago." If he'd held out for Erin, he could have saved himself some grief.

"If you had, I wouldn't have seen it. I've only been here a year, and when I arrived, I didn't look."

He understood. She hadn't been ready then. But had anything changed? What made him think she was any more ready for commitment now than she'd been then?

What he'd done was dumb. She'd seemed disappointed when he'd said the kiss didn't mean anything. She'd even let him put his arm around her and hold her hand. But that was a far cry from committing to forever.

If only he could take her home and retrieve the key later. But it was too late. He'd already opened his big mouth.

He'd poured out his heart in that letter. Once she read what he wrote, their friendship would become uncomfortable. Actually, simple friendship had become impossible somewhere between fearing he was going to lose her in the fire and realizing he'd once again fallen in love with her. And that was why he'd written the letter. He'd always been an all-or-nothing kind of guy.

She stepped onto the platform next to the bent-over palm and stretched, raising herself onto her toes. After sliding her fingers into a few of the recesses between the bases of the metal fronds, she eyed him with a frown.

"There'd better not be any spiders in here. Whose idea was this, anyway?"

"Yours."

"Oh, yeah."

Moments later she stepped down, arm raised in triumph, the key clutched in her hand. His own had grown clammy. His pulse had taken on an erratic rhythm, and the food he'd eaten had congealed into a doughy lump.

He swallowed hard. "I'll wait here."

That was the arrangement. One would leave the note; the other would digest it in privacy and decide how and whether to respond.

Of course, if her answer wasn't what he'd hoped it would be, the ride back to Fort Myers would be really uncomfortable. He hadn't thought that part through.

She handed him Alcee's leash. She wouldn't need his truck. The post office was at the edge of the park. "I'll be back." She bounded away from him at a half jog.

Some of his tension dissipated. Maybe he wasn't making a mistake. Erin had to have an idea of what was in his letter. If she had no desire for a romantic relationship, there would be some stiffness in her step.

He moved up the sidewalk and strolled the length of the parking lot, Alcee trotting beside him. Then he turned and did it again. Three times, and Erin still hadn't appeared.

That was good, right? That meant she was thinking about it rather than giving him a firm, reactive *no*.

He changed direction once again. No, it wasn't good. The fact she had to think about it at all meant she wasn't ready. And the longer she thought about it, the more reasons she'd come up with for why a romantic relationship was a bad idea.

He'd jumped the gun. He should've waited, given her more time to get used to the idea of allowing what they had to progress beyond friendship. Now he'd blown it.

He dropped to one knee and cupped the dog's face between his hands.

"Oh, Alcee, what have I done?"

Erin leaned against the brick facade of the post office, a single sheet of paper clutched in one sweaty hand. Her heart pounded, and she was having a hard time drawing in a full breath.

Cody had done it. He'd gotten a post office box and written a letter. And she was on the verge of a full-blown panic attack.

She had to give him an answer. She could tell him she needed more time. He'd give it to her. But that wouldn't be fair to Cody. She knew herself. The decision would hang over her like a piece of nasty unfinished business, the dread building, making it impossible to ever say yes. *God, please show me what to do. Whatever decision I make, please let it be the right one.*

She reached for her phone. Her purse was in Cody's truck, tucked under the passenger seat, but she'd slipped her phone into her back pocket. It was a good thing, because she really needed to talk to Courtney. Courtney would know how to talk her off the ledge.

No. She slid her phone back into her pocket. She couldn't call a friend when she was out on a date with Cody.

She pushed herself away from the wall and started to pace. Yes, she could. Even *Who Wants to Be a Mil-*

lionaire allowed phone-a-friend. She could actually see some correlation between her situation and the popular game show. The stakes were astronomical. She could be blissfully happy with her all-time true love, or she could crash and burn, like all the other times.

She pulled up Courtney's number in her contacts and pressed the call icon. Courtney was her sounding board. More than that, she was her lifeline. Actually, wasn't that what they called the helpers on the game show?

When her friend answered, Erin skipped the greeting. "You gotta help me. I think I'm going to hyperventilate."

"Slow down and take some deep breaths." For the next several moments Courtney did exactly that, sending the sounds of heavy, controlled breathing through the phone. Erin closed her eyes and joined her friend.

"Now, tell me what's going on."

Erin took a final deep breath. "It's Cody."

"Is he all right?" Courtney's tone held a note of alarm. "I thought the case was over."

"It is." She lowered her voice. "He wrote the letter."

"What does it say?"

She held the piece of paper under the glow emanating from the overhead lighting. Somehow, reading the words aloud seemed like being untrue to Cody. But she couldn't do this alone. She cleared her throat.

"'Erin, I'm better at building things than composing poetic words, but I'm going to give it my best shot. I was reminded recently that God works in mysterious ways. Our paths didn't cross by accident. I believe God used circumstances to bring us together.'"

"See, what did I tell you?"

Erin smiled at the interruption, which was exactly

what she'd expected to hear from Courtney. "'When I left Chicago for a warmer climate, I chose here, hoping you'd found your way back, too, or would eventually. Everything I felt for you so long ago was still there. Now it consumes me. I love you and want you to be a part of my life forever.'"

She lowered the page. There was more, language that was typical Cody—concern and understanding for everything she'd been through, the desire to be there for her. He'd ended by begging her to let down her guard and trust him with her heart. But it was the last sentence she'd read to Courtney that had her thoughts spinning and panic coursing through her. Cody loved her and wanted her to be a part of his life forever.

Courtney was silent for several moments. "And you're having trouble making a decision."

"Of course I'm having trouble with the decision. Forever is a long time."

"You love him, right?"

"I never said that."

"You don't have to. You talk about him every time we run, and there's emotion behind every word."

Yeah, she loved him. She'd been fighting it almost from the moment they'd pulled him out of the rubble. She began to pace again, and her gaze fell on one of the windows. Inside, the box Cody had rented was wide-open, the key still in the lock. She walked back through the glass door.

Courtney didn't force her to answer the first question before she moved on to the second. "Are there any red flags?"

"None yet. But I'm good at missing those until it's too late."

"From the times I've talked to Cody and everything you've told me about him, I'm not sensing any land mines." A sigh came through the phone. "Life is filled with uncertainty. Sometimes you have to be willing to take some risks to get the rewards."

Erin closed the box and pocketed the key. She didn't like risks, especially when it came to her heart. She was sure Cody was everything she believed him to be. But what if she was wrong? It wouldn't be the first time. Or even the second or third.

Worse yet, what if she committed to him, made promises, then found she couldn't follow through? She knew what her leaving had done to him the first time. If she did it again, how long would it take him to pick up the pieces? She couldn't do that to someone as sweet and selfless as Cody.

"Have you prayed about it?" Courtney's tone was sympathetic.

"Yes. But before tonight my prayers were to help me guard my heart and not be hurt again." Out loud, the words had a selfish ring. She turned around to face the bank of boxes, letting her head rest against one of them. "I can't bring myself to say no, though. I don't know if I can commit to what he's asking for, but I'm afraid that if I walk away again, I won't get another chance. And I believe that's something I'd regret for the rest of my life."

"It sounds like you might have just made your decision."

The tightness in her chest fled, coming out in a relaxed smile. Yes, she'd made her decision. She would risk anything to love and be loved by Cody. Even her heart.

She thanked Courtney and ended the call. When she

turned toward the door, two figures stood at the bank of windows. Her heart fluttered as Cody walked through the front door leading Alcee. His eyes were filled with hesitation. When she held out her hand, the hesitation turned to hope.

"I'm sorry I had to think about this so long."

One side of his mouth lifted. "You had me worried. I think I wore down the asphalt with my pacing."

"I'll admit, I had to phone a friend. I hope you don't mind."

"That depends on what you and your friend came up with."

She pulled her hand free and wrapped both arms around his neck, still clutching his letter. "I think you'll be happy with my answer."

His concern dissolved in a broad smile as his arms circled her waist. The joy in his eyes confirmed she was making the right decision.

"I'll be honest." She drew in a deep breath. "The thought of making a commitment like this scares me silly. All my adult life, I've been so determined to not end up where my mom is, having to get my dad's permission for everything she wants to do. So I always tried to keep my relationships casual. Sometimes that worked. Sometimes it didn't. But after ten years of dealing with losers and users, I'd decided I was through. From here on out, it was going to be just me and Alcee."

He gave her a crooked smile. "Alcee *is* pretty good company. She's not a bad conversationalist, either."

Erin grinned. "She's a better companion than a lot of men I've met."

"I hope you're not including me in that group."

"You're the exception to the rule." She once again

grew serious. "As much as the idea of commitment scares me, the thought of living the rest of my life without you is unbearable. I love you, Cody, and I'm so glad you didn't give up on me."

He tightened his embrace. "I love you, too. Now that there's not a burning building ready to collapse around us, can we try that kiss again?"

She grinned. "I think that's a great idea."

He dipped his head, and she met him halfway, rising up on her toes. When his lips met hers, her eyes fluttered shut, and she relaxed into him. This time there was no fear or desperation. Just an all-consuming sense of contentment. This was where she belonged.

At Alcee's bark, he pulled away. "I think she's being protective."

"No, she's being jealous. Neither of us is paying attention to her."

She cupped the dog's face in her hands and scratched her cheeks. "You're spoiled. You know that?"

When she straightened, he drew her into his embrace again. The fluorescents above them bathed their stark surroundings in harsh white light. Not the dreamiest setting. But anywhere with Cody was romantic.

She laid her head against his chest. "This is a big step for me, but I recognize what you had to go through to get to this point. Letting down your guard enough to trust that I won't walk away like your mother and your wife couldn't have been easy. I decided if you're willing to face your fears, then I could find the courage to face mine."

"I'm glad you did." He moved his hand up her back and entwined his fingers in her hair. "So does this mean you'll marry me?"

"No."

His arms fell, and he stepped back, brows drawn together. "Why not?"

"Because you haven't asked."

Relief spilled out in laughter. "I can remedy that." He took both of her hands and dropped to one knee. "Erin Jeffries, will you marry me?"

"If you give me a little time to get used to the idea, yes."

He rose, wrapped her in a sideways hug and led her toward the door. "You can have all the time you need."

When they reached the parking lot, he opened the back passenger door of his truck. Alcee hopped in and stretched across the seat.

Erin nodded in her direction. "That's our ring bearer there."

"Absolutely. From what I've seen, she'll have no problem learning how to walk down an aisle carrying a silk pillow."

Cody opened her door, and she climbed in, shaking her head.

"What?"

"I can't believe you asked me to marry you in a post office lobby."

"Hey, this all started with you digging me out of rubble."

She slid both arms around his neck. "I guess we don't do anything normally."

"You never have." He leaned in to kiss her on the tip of the nose. "And I love you for it."

* * * * *

*If you enjoyed this exciting story of suspense and
intrigue, pick up these other stories
from Carol J. Post:*

Buried Memories
Reunited by Danger
Fatal Recall
Lethal Legacy
Bodyguard for Christmas
Dangerous Relations

Available now from Love Inspired Suspense!

Find more great reads at www.LoveInspired.com.

Dear Reader,

I hope you've enjoyed Erin and Cody's story. This is my first book featuring a search-and-rescue dog, and I had a great time researching how they're trained and what they do. The real Alcee, a white German shepherd belonging to my critique partner, Sabrina, greets me warmly every time I arrive for plotting/writing retreats.

Cody and Erin were fun characters for me to write. Erin went through some trauma that left her with nightmares. Although she'd prayed for them to stop, she had to instead accept that God's grace is sufficient. Sometimes He removes the "thorn"; other times He uses it to teach us trust. Erin wasn't the only one with lessons to learn. Both she and Cody carried a lot of baggage and had to work through those issues to find their happily-ever-after.

May God richly bless you in all you do.

Love in Christ,
Carol J. Post

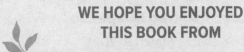

Get 4 FREE REWARDS!

We'll send you 2 FREE Books plus 2 FREE Mystery Gifts.

Love Inspired Suspense books showcase how courage and optimism unite in stories of faith and love in the face of danger.

FREE Value Over $20

SPECIAL EXCERPT FROM

LOVE INSPIRED SUSPENSE
INSPIRATIONAL ROMANCE

*When search-and-rescue park ranger Autumn Mercer
and her K-9 partner, Sherlock, meet a stranger in the
mountains whose brother has gone missing, they drop
everything to join the search. But with a storm and
gunmen closing in, can she and Derek Peterson survive
long enough to complete their mission?*

Read on for a sneak preview of
Mountain Survival *by Christy Barritt,*
available March 2021 from Love Inspired Suspense.

After another bullet whizzed by, Autumn turned, trying
to get a better view of the gunman. She had to figure out
where he was.

"Stay behind the tree," she whispered to Derek. "And
keep an eye on Sherlock."

Finally, she spotted a gunman crouched behind a
nearby boulder. The front of his Glock was pointed at her.

A Glock? The man definitely wasn't a hunter.

Autumn already knew that, though.

Hunters didn't aim their guns at people.

Her gaze continued to scan the area. She spotted
another man behind a tree and a third man behind another
boulder.

Who were these guys? And what did they want from
Autumn?

Backup couldn't get here soon enough.

The breeze picked up again, bringing another smattering of rain with it. They didn't have much time here. The conditions were going to become perilous at any minute. The storm might drive the gunman away, but it would present other dangers in the process.

She spotted a fourth man behind another tree in the distance. They all surrounded the campsite where Derek and his brother had set up.

They'd been waiting for Derek to return, hadn't they?

Why? What sense did that make?

She didn't have time to think about that now. Another bullet came flying past, piercing a nearby tree.

"What are we going to do?" Derek whispered. "Can I help?"

"Just stay behind a tree and remain quiet," she said. "We don't want to make this too easy for them."

Sherlock let out a little whine, but Autumn shushed the dog.

The man fired again. This time the bullet split the wood only inches from her.

Autumn's heart raced. These men were out for blood.

Even if the men ran out of bullets, she and Derek were going to be outnumbered. They couldn't just wait here for that to happen.

She had to act—and now.

She turned, pulling her gun's trigger.

Don't miss
Mountain Survival *by Christy Barritt,*
available March 2021 wherever Love Inspired Suspense books and ebooks are sold.

LoveInspired.com

LOVE INSPIRED

INSPIRATIONAL ROMANCE

UPLIFTING STORIES OF FAITH, FORGIVENESS AND HOPE.

Join our social communities to connect with other readers who share your love!

Sign up for the Love Inspired newsletter at **LoveInspired.com** to be the first to find out about upcoming titles, special promotions and exclusive content.

CONNECT WITH US AT:

Facebook.com/LoveInspiredBooks

Twitter.com/LoveInspiredBks

Facebook.com/groups/HarlequinConnection

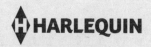
HARLEQUIN

Heartfelt or thrilling, passionate or uplifting—Harlequin is more than just happily-ever-after.

With twelve different series to choose from and new books available every month, you are sure to find stories that will move you, uplift you, inspire and delight you.